The Year _the_

Eric Campbell has spent most of his _____ in
the tropics, mainly in _____ Guinea, where he
lived at the foot of an _____
and in East Africa, w
of Mount Kilimanjar__

He now lives in Nor_____
but plans to travel abroad again _____

Also by
Eric Campbell in Piper
The Place of Lions

Eric Campbell

The Year of the
Leopard Song

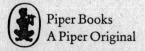

Piper Books
A Piper Original

The extract from 'The Snows of Kilimanjaro' by Ernest Hemingway
from *The First Forty-Nine Stories* is reproduced
by kind permission of the Estate of Ernest Hemingway and
Jonathan Cape, London; and of the Hemingway Foreign Rights
Trust, Copyright © 1936, all rights outside U.S., Hemingway
Foreign Rights Trust, and Macmillan Publishing Co Inc, USA.

The extract from the book *Kilimanjaro* by John Reader is
reproduced by kind permission of Hamish Hamilton.

First published 1992 by
Pan Books Ltd, Cavaye Place, London SW10 9PG

9 8 7 6 5 4 3 2 1

© Eric Campbell 1992

ISBN 0 330 32408 X

Printed in England by Clays Ltd, St Ives plc

For my son Jeremy,
who knows Kilimanjaro
better than I do

'Kilimanjaro is a snow-covered mountain nineteen thousand, seven hundred and ten feet high and is said to be the highest mountain in Africa. Its western summit is called, by the Maasai, Ngàje Ngài – the House of God. Close to the western summit is the dried and frozen carcass of a leopard.

No one has explained what the leopard was seeking at that altitude.'

Ernest Hemingway, *The Snows of Kilimanjaro*

'The plains below distant Mawenzi were once the home of Ernest Hemingway. In his book *The Snows of Kilimanjaro* he immortalized this rocky outcrop, Leopard Point. So called because, in the 1920s, the frozen corpse of a leopard was photographed there.

Why had it climbed to its nemesis in this primordial landscape, where no animal can survive the night unaided?

No one knows. But in a cleft in the rocks, close to the roof of Africa, the leopard has its final resting place, its bones embedded in ice.

Like a sacrifice to the superior force of the mountain.'

John Reader, *Kilimanjaro*

one

'Ladies and gentlemen, we will shortly be landing at Nairobi International Airport. The seat-belt sign is now illuminated so would you please return to your seats, fasten your seat-belts and refrain from smoking until in the airport terminal. The local time is seven-thirty a.m. and the ground temperature is sixty-five degrees. Thank you for flying Kenyan Airways.'

Alan Edwards breathed a deep sigh of relief. Nearly home at last. Night flights were purgatory and this one had been worse than most. He had only just fallen into a cramped and painful sleep somewhere over Europe when a bout of turbulence had crashed and bumped him awake again, and after that he had been unable to settle. The night had been very long thereafter, with nothing to do but eat too many meals and stare at the back of the seat in front. And there had been a baby crying for most of the night, setting everyone's teeth on edge.

But at least it was now all over. The flight was over; but much, much more importantly the year was over too.

It had seemed like a good idea at the time, going to school in England. It had seemed a great adventure.

'The boy ought to go home to do his "A" Levels,'

his father had said. 'He spends far too much time driving around the bush on that blasted motor bike to do any studying here. We'll send him home to school for a year.'

A funny thing, Alan reflected, that all the expatriates in Africa referred to England as 'home', spoke lovingly and endlessly of green fields, country pubs and crisp, frosty mornings, yet never seemed to go there. Or, if they did, they soon came back. Now he knew why. England, he had decided, washes the life from you. England drains the colour from your skin, hunches your shoulders under the weight of accumulated drizzle and encloses you in a prison of claustrophobia with its teeming people and killer traffic. He'd only needed a very tiny space to himself in England, but he hadn't been able to find it.

School had been tolerable, but how homesick he had been for Africa and its freedom and its huge crystal skies. How he longed for the silence of the plains and the warm, spiced breezes blowing in from the Indian Ocean.

The plane slowed and began to bank, turning on to its final landing path. Alan looked down on to Nairobi sprawling away into the distance, its concrete and glass white and shimmering in the early morning sunlight. 'Green City in the Sun' the road signs say as you drive in, and from the air you can see why. It is a city of spaces and parks, a city that has remembered that people need grass to retain sanity amidst tower blocks. Huge slabs of green were dotted around the city, and even from this height Alan could see that the jacaranda trees were in full flower, their purple blossoms tracing delicate paint lines around the park edges. In the gardens of the neat suburban houses the white frangipani blooms winked in the light and scarlet hibiscus and purple bougainvillea hedges clashed startlingly with the pastel painted walls.

The morning rush would be on now as thousands of irritable commuters fought their way to work: the rich in their cars, driven half-mad by traffic jams, other incensed drivers and ill-tempered vindictive policemen; the poor crammed into open-backed dilapidated trucks which roared into town in great clouds of blue smoke; and those who simply walked, the thousands who pad the dusty roads radiating in from the city's edges, unable even to pay the truck-fare.

The engine speed increased slightly signalling that they were about to land, and a few seconds later the plane's huge wheels thumped on to the runway.

Home. Back to Africa.

The plane thundered down the runway, gradually slowed and then turned off on to its taxiing path. The anxious tourists started to get their bags from the overhead lockers and stand worriedly in the aisles as though, should they delay, Africa would leave without them.

Alan wondered who would be there to meet him. The farm would be very busy at the moment; it was harvesting time for the coffee and his father might not have been able to get away. Probably one of the plantation workers would have come for him.

The plane came to a halt. Alan stood and gathered

together his hand-luggage, waiting patiently for the doors to open. He longed, in the air-conditioned cool of the plane, for the first smell of the warm breath of Africa blowing in from the dry savannahs; the smell of red earth and time. He longed for the quiet mornings of the farm and the cheery calls and giggles of the women harvesting the coffee. And to see again the great grazing herds of zebra and wildebeest, elephant moving like boulders through the trees, the quick, dancing gazelles.

The doors bumped open and he found himself pressed along in the push of people anxious to put their feet back where they belonged; on the earth.

On the tarmac he escaped the jostling line of tourists and paused to take in the moment. The morning was clear and the sun already dazzling. He stood, luxuriating in the touch of the sun on his skin. He breathed deeply and gratefully of the scent of Africa. A soft breeze was blowing in from the Kapiti Plain and for Alan it carried memory on its breath; the acrid tang of acacia and loping giraffe; warm mist rising from lonely sand-rivers; the smoke of cattle-dung fires; the sharp stench of lion and sweetness of sighing grass. The smell of the highveldt, the drug which draws all travellers back to Africa.

Even in those first few seconds of his return Alan felt strength flood into him. The sun and the warm breeze quickened his blood and lightened his shoulders. He felt his mind beginning to clear of the interminable trivia of the past year and slow to the pace of Africa. All around him tourists, unaware that time is flexible in Africa, were becoming impatient

4

with baggage handlers and customs officers. They were upsetting only themselves; patience is not a virtue in Africa, it is a way of life.

The immigration officer smiled at Alan as he stamped his passport.

'Jambo, bwana. Habari?'

How good it was to hear Swahili again.

Alan grinned. 'Mzuri,' he replied. 'I'm fine. Now.' And he made his way through Immigration and out into the concourse.

It was very crowded and very noisy. He craned his neck to scan over the crowds, looking for a familiar face. Seeing no one he recognized he passed through the concourse and emerged, blinking, on to the airport access road. His father's Land-Rover was parked about a hundred yards down the road, a tall, black young man sitting on the bonnet. The last person Alan had expected to be here was waiting for him.

He was overjoyed. It was Kimathi, son of their house-servant Njombo. The Chagga boy Alan had grown up with; the boy he thought of as his brother.

'Kim,' he shouted. 'Kimathi. Over here.'

The young man jumped down from the Land-Rover and strode towards Alan, a grin splitting his face from ear to ear.

'Bwana Alan,' he bellowed happily. 'Karibu. Karibu sana. Welcome. Welcome home.'

'Kim. How good to see you. But how did you get here? Who's with you. Who drove?'

'I drove, bwana. I can drive now. Last year your father taught me, while you were away. On the day

I was eighteen he bought me my licence. So, last night I have driven from Marangu to here. I slept in the cab so I would not be late for you.'

He gathered up Alan's bags and together they walked back to the Land-Rover.

'Everyone waits to see you, Bwana Alan. We have all missed you. Come, climb in, we have a long way to go and everyone waits for you.'

They clambered into the cab.

'Now I will see how well you drive,' said Alan, as Kimathi started the engine. 'If my father taught you, you will drive too fast and dangerously, like him.' They both laughed, for John Edwards's driving was a legend.

Alan watched as Kimathi revved the engine slightly, released the handbrake, placed his left hand on the gear lever and engaged first gear.

And because he had grown up with this boy, because he was so accustomed to him, because his every feature was as familiar to him as his own, Alan did not notice any more the strange, genetic trick which had given the hand he was watching five fingers and one thumb.

two

The old man who watched over the tree sent for Kimathi early in the morning while the pale sunrise still fingered through the cold ghost-mists of dawn.

The village was silent with sleep and in those first, numbed moments of awakening he was reluctant to leave the dark, protective warmth of the hut.

He lay for a while, looking up at the smoke-blackened thatch of the roof. Tiny rustlings came from deep inside it as the quick, bright lizards who were its permanent occupants settled themselves again, grumbling at the early morning call. Wisps of smoke still rose from the dying fire in the hut's centre, curling lazily into the thatch and creeping through the hole in the roof which now seeped morning light down to where he lay.

He turned on to his side and looked around. The others were all still asleep, undisturbed by the whispered, urgent message that the old man's runner had brought. His older brothers breathed deeply and rhythmically, huddled in their soft animal-skin blankets around the edges of the hut. Njombo, his father, wheezed restlessly on his raised pallet with its comfortable mattress of dried grasses. Ageing now, and fearing the cold of the nights, his bed was in the centre, close to the fire. In the adjoining room, where his mother and sisters slept, he could hear a voice murmuring, its owner still asleep.

He rose quietly and, with careful feet, crossed the floor of the hut. He pulled back the curtain of beaten bark which hung at the doorway and stepped outside.

It was very cold, and a moaning wind poured down from the high glaciers carrying ice on its breath. It scoured across the village; a surgical wind, cutting. The cloud was very low on the mountain, he noticed. High on the tops snow would be piling on eternal snow.

He pulled his coarse, woollen blanket close around him, hunched his shoulders against the wind and shuffled, barefoot, across the dusty clearing at the village centre. The huts circled him blackly in the morning half-light, the ground they stood on still hidden in a white cotton wool of mist. They looked baseless, unanchored, as though the crying wind could float them away on the white sea. Behind them, far, far in the distance, the rearing spires and fangs of Mawenzi had torn holes through the clouds and soared in stark silhouette against the lightening sky.

He shuddered as he passed between the huts on the far side of the clearing and emerged on to the path which led down to the old man's cave. A shudder not just from the cold but from the fear building in his stomach.

The call had not been unexpected. One day it had had to come, he had always known that. But he had preferred to keep it out of his mind. From the earliest days of his childhood he had been told about this day; been told the story of what it was that set him apart and of what it was he must do.

At first it had meant little to him. Then, briefly, he had been proud that he was different.

Finally he had cursed it for what it did to his life and for what it would do to him to the end of his days.

He had learned it gradually as he had grown. Learned that the other children, though they accepted him into their games and rituals, were wary of him; even fearful, he sometimes thought. In the middle of some happy, headlong game he would find them staring at his footprints in the dust and shaking their heads with wonder. And he would run back to his hut, crying with humiliation.

From all the children he had played with as a child he had no close friend; no other child had ever taken him to its heart. Except one – and he was not of his kind.

As the years had passed from childhood into puberty he had watched as the other boys of his age found girlfriends and shyly whispered secrets and held their hands in the shadows of the huts. But the girls avoided him, were uneasy in his presence, and he soon realized that no girl would ever be his.

Now he was accustomed, in his eighteenth year, to live expecting isolation and cursing his luck that he had been the one singled out. The one to bear the mark.

The six fingers and toes of his hands and feet had sealed his fate from the day he had entered the world, when, within minutes, the excited villagers had gathered around his hut to glimpse him and the Watcher of the Tree had been told of his arrival.

And now the day was here. The call could mean only one thing. The Song had begun again, and the Watcher of the Tree was hearing it and making his preparations.

The boy continued along the path, winding his way down the hillside, still huddled against the cold.

The path was well-known. He had trodden it a thousand times bringing food down from the village for the old man.

And a thousand times he had sat in the warm glow of the cave-fire and heard the story told and retold, the cave and time giving it a magic resonance.

The story of the Song was as familiar to him as breath.

There was no welcoming glow from the cave-mouth today as he looked down. The grey boulders of the small outcrop rose out of the swirling mist like the heads of great, prehistoric sea-monsters bubbling through the surface of a smoking sea. Behind them reared the tree, its huge arms reaching out over the rocks like a witch conjuring spirits from a cauldron.

The boy paused and looked hard at the tree, seeking a change in its appearance. As yet there was none to be seen, but if the Song had begun then change must come. His life and the lives of all the Chagga tribe were bound to it.

His heart lurched at the thought.

He carried on down the hillside. As he neared the rocks he could see that the old man was standing outside the cave, his head turned upwards peering into the dense cloudbank which hid the great dome of Kibo. He stood like an ancient biblical prophet, thin and erect, his grey hair glistening with moisture from the cold mist, his earth-red robe a vivid wound of colour in the drab morning light.

The boy called out as he approached so as not to startle the old man.

'Jambo, mzee.'

The old man shook his head in annoyance, then continued his motionless vigil until the boy arrived to stand quietly by his side.

They stood for long minutes in silence. The wind moaned eerily through the crevices of the rocks and the dark tree branches.

The old man's eyes remained fixed on a single point in the cloud, as though he could see through its denseness to a point deep within; as though his eyes bored a tunnel of light through the grey, and illuminated the slopes of the hidden peak.

Finally he spoke the words the boy had known he would hear.

'So,' he said, 'it is beginning. I have heard the Song.'

The boy turned his head upwards to the mountain, seeing in his mind the jagged, thrusting rocks of Leopard Point. The place from which the magic of the Song flowed.

'Yes,' he replied.

'Soon it will sing to you. Soon your journey must begin.'

'Yes,' said Kimathi, still staring up at the mountain.

Soon he must go up there, into the snows of Kilima Njaro, the White Mountain. To the roof of all Africa.

To the place of the Song.

And so it began.

An old man and a boy on the threshold of the year they were to call the Year of the Leopard Song.

three

It started with a few minor incidents that Alan, in the excitement of his first days home, hardly even noticed, or attached no significance to if he did. His homecoming was too long-awaited and too welcome for anything to intrude.

But now his father had said something and he was forced to think.

'There's something going on out there,' John Edwards had said that morning. 'I can feel it in my bones.'

Alan had groaned inwardly and his mother, Mary, had smiled gently and said, 'Yes, dear, of course.'

They were both well accustomed to John Edwards's 'bones', which, over the years, had been able to predict the weather, the world economy, the movement of shipping and even what government policy would be before the government knew it.

'The rains will come early this year, I can feel it in my bones.'

'Yes, Dad.'

'The price of coffee's going to fall, I can feel it in my bones.'

'Yes, dear, of course you can.'

'There'll be a tanker in Dar es Salaam soon. We'll have petrol again, I can feel it . . .'

'Yeah, yeah.'

'The government will put a stop to that. You'll see. I can . . .'

'Sure, Dad, you're quite right.'

Looking back over the years though, those who scoffed at him might have had to admit grudgingly to themselves, though never of course to him, that he was nearly always right.

'You can laugh,' he said that morning as they sat at breakfast on the cool veranda of the house. 'You can laugh. But you mark my words, there's something funny going on. Listen. Tell me what you hear.'

Alan listened.

A clatter of dishes came from the kitchen as Njombo washed up last night's dinner things. He heard the soft whoosh of a grass broom as a servant swept the polished wood floors of the house and the odd, clear calls of morning birds from the damp forests rising behind the coffee slopes. Tiny noises in an immense silence.

'It's too quiet. It's been like this for over a week now.'

'Oh, nonsense, John,' said Alan's mother, starting to stack the breakfast dishes noisily on to a tray. 'Everybody's working hard on the harvest. People are getting tired, that's all.'

She furrowed her brow slightly and glared at her husband. Alan noticed the look. Despite her reassuring words she obviously agreed with him.

14

Things *were* too quiet, Alan had to admit it. Always, before he had gone away, his alarm clock had been the workers arriving at dawn on the slopes, calling out the day's news, holding conversations at half a mile's distance in high, happy bellows and clear peals of laughter. The well-remembered, much-loved background music to his life.

And now it was missing. In the excitement of his arrival home and the heady first few days of rediscovering the farm, Alan hadn't given it more than a passing thought. But his parents were obviously uneasy and that made him uneasy too.

'It's probably nothing,' he ventured. 'They'll be brewing up to asking you for a raise in pay.'

His mother nodded in agreement.

'Yes, dear, I'm sure you're right.'

She glared again at her husband but he was too preoccupied with his thoughts to notice.

'No, it's not that. It's something more than that. I asked Njombo what was going on, but he wouldn't say. He just muttered something about "a problem". He wouldn't give any more than that. "A village problem, bwana." The thing is, when he said it he looked, I don't know, guilty I suppose is the only word. He wouldn't look me in the eye.'

'That's not like Njombo,' Alan replied, incredulous. 'He's the most gentle, honest person there is. What could he possibly have to be guilty about?'

'Don't ask me. All I know is what my bones are telling me. And they're telling me something's happening.'

He scowled at the garden as though it were its fault.

Alan's mother picked up the tray and swirled abruptly away into the house. She was obviously cross and that added to the unease Alan was beginning to feel. His father ignored her exit.

'And there's another thing,' he added. 'Your pal Kimathi. I sent him down to Moshi a couple of days ago with the invoices for the Coffee Authority. He was gone six hours. Six hours. When I asked him what he'd been doing he said he'd been queueing for petrol for four hours but didn't manage to get any.'

'Well, that's nothing new. We've all done that. The pump always runs out two cars in front of us.'

'I know. It's not the story that makes me suspicious, it's the way he told it. Like Njombo, he didn't look me in the eye. I knew it wasn't true.'

'That's funny, I've never known Kim to lie. It's not in his nature. Perhaps he's got a girlfriend and he's too embarrassed to say.'

'Hm, perhaps. Anyway he hasn't turned up yet this morning so you might just bike down to the village and see what he's up to. See if you can get a clue to what's going on. I'm off to work.'

He pushed his bush-hat irascibly down on to his head, stumped down the veranda steps and disappeared through the untidy banana plants on his way to the roasting-sheds.

Alan sat and reflected quietly. His father was right, of course, and Alan was forced now to admit some things to himself.

On the surface the farm, and all the people on

it, had been just as he remembered. Kimathi had welcomed him back like the long-lost brother he nearly was. Kimathi's father, Njombo, who had been the family house-servant since long before Alan was born, had fussed around him like a long, black hen, squeezing his arms and shaking his head in dismay at the boy's thinness, and weeping a little with happiness at his return. All the farm workers he had met on the coffee slopes had greeted him with a smile and a cheery, 'Karibu, bwana', and seemed glad to see him back.

And as he had walked the quiet, red-earth roads, soaking in the sun and relearning the peace of Africa, the villagers and the village children had greeted him with the quiet warmth he had expected.

Yet there was something which had changed.

The surface remained the same, but below the surface were things that made him pause: the figure, seen from the distance, who turned off his path as he saw Alan approach; the door which closed too abruptly as he strode into the village; the man who greeted him with a smile on his face but not in his eyes.

Tiny things, yes. Dismissed as unimportant at the time, but noted and stored.

At home, too. He had wandered into the kitchen one morning to find Njombo in whispered conversation with another man at the kitchen door. Nothing unusual in that, people came to the door at all times of day. But the man had left immediately after Alan had greeted him, and Njombo had thereafter looked at the dishes he washed with more than usual

17

concentration . . . Or he had looked at the floor, or the walls, or out of the window. Anywhere except at Alan.

And, most important and baffling of all, since the day he had collected him at Nairobi Airport, Kimathi had not once been to the house to see him. He had come to work, done the jobs allotted to him and gone home.

'This is silly,' Alan said to himself, pulling out of the reverie. 'It's my father and his blessed bones putting ideas into my head. The answer's simple. I've been away. I can't expect everyone to fall all over me just because I'm back. They've all got their own lives to lead. They're just shy. They think England will have changed me, and they're a bit wary of me, that's all. Nothing to worry about.'

But he didn't really convince himself. Things weren't right and inside himself he knew it.

Anyway, it was no use sitting and puzzling about it. If something was happening then something was happening. There were things out there, beyond the farm fence, which no expatriate could ever know about; not even one like him who had been born here and lived almost all his days here. Africans extended the warm hand of friendship to pull you in, but they didn't pull you in all the way. Only as far as they wanted you to come. Some doors would always remain closed though you knocked on them to the end of time.

Some things were simply not for the white man to know.

Alan shrugged the thoughts off. Why spoil the

happiness of his homecoming with things which would probably not concern him?

'A village problem,' Njombo had said.

It was probably a fight with another village; someone would have stolen someone's cow, or someone's girl, and everyone was upset and vengeful. In time things would adjust. Kimathi would turn up at the door one day and they would go clattering off on the dusty bush-tracks on the motor bike, swim in the Marangu Falls, walk the mountain paths and mimic the chatters of the Colobus monkeys in the high, rain-forest trees of Kilima Njaro, just as they always had done. Things would get back to normal.

Alan rose from the cane armchair and made his way into the house, passing through the french windows into the dimness of the living room. The walls were hung with trophies from his father's hunting days and eyes stared down at him from all the walls. A water buffalo gazed intimidatingly across the room at a gazelle, a lion glared down at a cheetah, a kudu stared blankly at a leopard. He looked around them with distaste. They had fascinated and frightened him when he was young and he had thrilled to the stories of the hunt and the kill. Now he preferred to see creatures alive, not in the fixed, featureless gaze of death.

He made his way through the house to the kitchen. He was going to ask Njombo where Kimathi was, but he was no longer there. Probably he was down at the shamba gathering vegetables for dinner, or collecting eggs from the chicken pen.

No matter, Alan would go down to the village and seek Kim out there.

He wandered out of the back door into the garden and looked up at the mountain. The cloud was still low, obscuring the peaks. It hadn't cleared since he came back and he was longing to see the huge, white dome of Kibo again.

His mother was down at the end of the garden quietly snipping flowers and placing them carefully into her basket. Alan watched her for a moment. She was uneasy, in spite of her protestations, that was obvious, and he wondered whether to walk down and question her. He decided against it. Whatever her worries were she wouldn't tell her son.

Instead he walked along the side of the house and turned the corner towards the shed where he kept his motor bike.

He was just in time, as he turned the corner, to catch sight of Njombo disappearing through the big eucalyptus trees on to the path which snaked down the mountainside to the village.

He called out.

'Njombo.'

The man's head turned very slightly, almost imperceptibly, at the call. There was no doubt that he had heard. But, strangely, he did not stop, did not even acknowledge the boy. He vanished into the trees.

Alan stood perplexed, wondering whether he should follow him. Then he shrugged, decided that Njombo must have something urgent on his mind and walked over to the shed to pull out his beloved Honda 125.

As always, the shed was a mess. Empty coffee sacks stood in huge, untidy piles; bits of old engines littered the shelves; spades, forks, scythes and machetes leaned in crazy bundles against the walls and against the piles of sacks. Everywhere was dust, and cobwebs so thick you had to fight them from your face.

Alan pulled the dust-sheet from his motor bike, took hold of the handlebars and started to drag the machine towards the door.

He manoeuvred it backwards and forwards a few times to get it lined up and, as he did so, the foot-rest caught against one of several planks of wood leaning against the workbench. The plank slipped sideways and fell against the next one, which fell against the next until, domino-like, they all fell with a huge clatter to the floor. The crash caused a cloud of acrid dust to rise up catching the back of Alan's throat, making him cough and splutter and temporarily blinding him.

Cursing, he held the heavy motor bike with one hand while he coughed the dust out of his lungs and rubbed his stinging eyes.

As his vision returned his throat caught again, this time with shock.

The planks had been hiding something. They had been placed there, carefully and deliberately, to hide something. Something which gripped Alan by the heart and froze him.

Suspended from the beams of the shed was the

carcass of a chicken. The head had been sliced cleanly off and tossed to one side; it lay near the edge of the bench, a single, open eye gleaming malevolently in death. The severed neck had dripped the lifeblood from the body until a sickening, red pool had formed on the workbench top, flowed out in channels of shocking scarlet and dripped on to the floor.

And behind the bench, on the wall, someone's finger had daubed, in large, coarse letters of blood, a single word.

CHUI.

Leopard!

four

It was a trick of the light which hid the entrance. Something about the angle the light entered the cave-mouth and bounced off the walls. It threw shadows, distorting and concealing the folds and cracks of the rock. Even in the glow of firelight the conformation, or the evenness of colour, of the rock had concealed the cleft from his eyes. He had never once noticed it, in all the years he had come to the cave.

So it was a shock when the old man said 'Come!', and seemed to walk through a solid wall and vanish.

But, when Kimathi followed, he found that the Watcher had merely turned into a cleft, entered a passage easily wide enough for a man, and was hobbling down a slope leading away into the darkness.

'Come,' he said again, melting into the gloom, 'It is time to make you ready.'

Kimathi went after him, a little fearfully.

The light from the cave-mouth soon faded away as he descended and he had to put his hands against the passage walls and feel his way carefully in the darkness. He could hear the old man's feet shuffling along, fading into the distance. The darkness had not slowed him at all; familiarity guided his feet surely.

Kimathi groped his way blindly along until gradually, after many twists and turns, the slope began to level and he could see faint light ahead once more. Soon it was enough for him to see the walls and floor of the passage and he could walk normally again.

He emerged into a second, hidden cave, where the old man, WaChui, waited for him.

The light here was very subdued, though Kimathi could see that this cave was much larger than the one they had left. They had descended deep into the earth, into a huge, rock cavern illuminated only by faint shafts of light seeping through cracks in the roof high above them. Their feet raised clouds of dust from the floor and it hung, dancing, in the light beams.

The floor was littered with large stones and boulders and WaChui had slumped heavily down on one.

'Now,' he said, 'we wait. And watch.'

Kimathi settled himself upon a stone and did as the old man said.

It was very cool and quiet down there. Faintly and distantly he could hear water trickling.

He looked around. The cave was not sinister or forbidding, though a different light may have made it so. As it was, the yellow rays of light seeping in from the cracks above gave it a peaceful air, like a dim, quiet church with evening light cracking and refracting through stained glass. A place where you felt you should whisper; a place with a presence which should not be disturbed. He could not see how far the cave extended, for the far end was swallowed in darkness. He felt that the wall was there, just beyond the limits of his vision. He stared hard into the velvet gloom but could see nothing.

They waited quietly for a long time. The soft afternoon wind sighed through the roof-cracks and Kimathi realized suddenly that the loudest sound in the cave was his own breathing. He was breathing too shallowly and too quickly.

He pulled himself up. He was nervous and it was showing. He consciously slowed his breath and quietened it, putting his hands together in his lap in case they should shake. Whatever it was they were waiting for he must show no fear.

He looked again at the old man, wondering whether to ask him what was going to happen. He decided against it, for he saw that the man's eyes were closed; not in sleep or rest, but in deep concentration. His head was slightly tilted as though his ears strained for a tiny, expected sound. Or as though his mind was boring into the darkness at the end of the cave.

Kimathi turned his eyes away from the old man. The beams of light in the roof shifted constantly as the sun moved across the sky. Like spotlights being switched off and on now some parts of the cave were lit, now others. As the sun faded at one entrance it brightened at another. And, as the minutes ticked by and the fierceness of the noon sun faded into afternoon, the light in the cave changed gradually from yellow-white, to yellow, to a deep, hazy gold.

The old man's eyes flicked open. His head turned, first to the left, then to the right. And back again.

His eyes moved rapidly from point to point on the walls, carefully noting where the light beams fell.

'Now,' he said. 'See.'

He pointed directly into the black void of darkness at the far end of the cave.

Kimathi looked. At first he saw nothing but blackness. He narrowed his eyes to help them adjust and saw that there was the faintest lightening penetrating the gloom. The angles of the beams were beginning to seep light into the edges of the pool of darkness, to creep along the side walls of the cave, revealing them, extending them, inch by inch. As the sun descended overhead so the light encroached further into the dark until the edges of the back wall began to be revealed. The centre however remained black and impenetrable, though it was to that which Kimathi's eyes were drawn.

He searched deep into the blackness. His heart was hammering in his chest and he could hear the pulsing blood thudding in his ears.

Something was there. He couldn't see it, he could feel it. Something stood in the dark pool, entirely motionless, looking out at him.

Still the light crept slowly, but with terrible inexorability, in from the cave sides, exposing more and more of the back wall. Still the centre remained malevolently black.

And then it happened.

As the sun lowered in the sky, a strange twist in the conformation of the rocks, a chance combination of the angles of the crevices and cracks and the way the sun's light hit them, closed all the places at which light had been penetrating and plunged the cave, with numbing suddenness, into complete darkness.

Kimathi sat, a petrified statue.

In the darkness WaChui began to intone in a low voice. At first the words were unintelligible, sounds only, but gradually they became louder and took meaning.

'The Leopard runs alone, run as the Leopard and
  hear its Song.
The Leopard kills in darkness, kill as the Leopard
  and be the Song.'

And as he chanted, the searching sun turned the rim of a rock high on the roof of the cave and shot a clear lance of light, a single, brilliant shaft of amber, into the darkness at the end of the cave.

Kimathi gasped at what the light revealed.

So superbly made, so delicately and carefully crafted, so realistic that in the first seconds of amazement he thought him to be alive, stood the figure of a Chagga warrior. Lit by the amber light, the ebony from which he was carved glinted like oiled skin. His head was raised upwards and turned slightly, his eyes gazing at the rock high on the cave side as though they saw through rock and earth to the immense heights of the mountain beyond. In the raised and bent right arm, its carved muscles almost seeming to ripple, he held a vicious hunting spear, slender and poised, its blade flashing like a faceted gem. The body leaned slightly, one foot forward, as though the warrior was on the point of hurling the spear at an invisible prey.

The amber light was taken up, intensified, by the leopard skins the warrior wore. A complete skin was draped over his head and hung down over his shoulders like a cloak. From the skull-less head of the animal glinted eyes fashioned from brilliant yellow scapolite. As the cave-light shifted, the black spots of the pelt seemed to move as though the long-gone body beneath was trying to reoccupy it. A second skin clothed the figure's body; a vivid tunic fastened at the shoulder with a yellow-stone pin and belted at the waist with a thin strip of fur. Around the biceps and wrists, the thighs and ankles, thick bands of fur swelled the warrior's muscles to fearsome size.

Kimathi exhaled, with an explosion of breath held for too long. The leopard-man of legend who had haunted his dreams, both waking and sleeping, since they had first told him the story, was here in front of him.

There was a long silence as the boy replaced dream with reality.

'So,' said the old man, very quietly. 'Now you must learn the Leopard's Song.'

'Yes.'

'Learn it well. My day is almost over. Soon the Leopard will sing only to you.'

'Yes.'

'Hear it and obey it.'

'I will hear it and obey it.'

Kimathi stood and began to walk towards the figure. All fear was gone. He knew exactly what he had to do now.

Quietly he removed the arm and leg bands and

fastened them on to himself. He slipped off his shirt and shorts and donned the tunic, fastening it carefully at the shoulder and knotting the belt tightly around his waist. The softness of the pelt felt good against his skin. It was warm and supple and the rich, animal smell of it pleased him. It smelled of the high plains and wind blowing; of the earth and rain and coarse grasses bruising underfoot. It smelled of the chase and clear skies and whirling trees.

And the blood of the kill.

He rubbed his hand along the fur. It was silky and very soft, though somehow charged with an electricity that tingled in his skin.

The old man took the caped head from the ebony figure and carefully placed it over Kimathi's head, arranging the skin neatly over his shoulders.

And finally Kimathi pulled the heavy, carefully fashioned paws from the carved hands and slipped his own hands into them.

The light was fading rapidly now. The single beam from the roof was gradually creeping up the walls and reddening as the sun began to set. In the last glimmers Kimathi, ready now, held up his right hand.

Enclosed in the leopard-skin glove his hand and arm felt suddenly stronger, more powerful.

He raised his hand higher, sliding it into the beam of light, and bunched his fist. His fingers pulled the fur in towards the palm, releasing the terrible, curved, metal claws which had been sewn into it generations ago.

And, of course, it was only another trick of the

light; only the redness pouring down the beam from the dying sun, glinting on the bright metal; but it seemed to the old man, as he looked up at the paw, that blood dripped from the viciously sharpened, murderous claws.

five

Whether it was the dawn light filtering down to his eyes from the cave roof which awoke him or whether it was the Song, Kimathi did not know. But the Song was there in his mind from the first moments of consciousness; a high, clear voice, sweetly melodic, pulsing with the rhythm of his heartbeat, calling him.

'Come,' the voice had said.

And he had followed.

WaChui, the Watcher of the Tree, was still asleep, so Kimathi left the cave without disturbing him.

Outside the air was cold and dank. Kimathi shuddered and pulled the leopard-skin cape around him to keep out the chill. He paused briefly, listening to the Song humming gently in his mind, waiting for it to give him direction. Above him the branches of the great tree which overhung the rocky outcrop hissed quietly in the morning wind and he looked up into them. He felt dwarfed by the tree, by its size and its immense age. There since the dawn of time, the story told, it had watched over change. It had seen Man take his first faltering footsteps and learn his place in this harsh land; watched the endless generations come and go with their joys and defeats, times of hunger and of plenty, of war and of peace.

And now Kimathi's life was bound up with this tree, as WaChui's had been before him, as had countless lives before his. For this was the Tree of Man, the tree from which all things Chagga came. Should this tree die, the story told, then the Chagga would die.

He gazed hard at the tree, searching among the paddle-shaped leaves for the first tiny swellings of the buds which would bring the yellow and black flowers they called leopard-heads. But there was nothing yet.

The Song was becoming louder in his head and he turned and looked up at the mountain. The voice was calling him upwards, from a point hidden by the clouds. He narrowed his eyes and stared into the greyness, trying to see where it would lead him. Then, as the insistent pulse of it increased, he began to move, drawn by its haunting sweetness, upwards on to the slopes of Kilima Njaro.

Soon he did not even notice where he was or where he was going. Everything faded but the Song. It guided him, turned him, pulled him, as though he followed a voice whose owner was always just out of sight, around the next corner, behind the next tree. It drew him steadily up the mountain slopes, past the wide track which snakes upwards from Mar-angu Gate to the climbers' huts of Mandara, and deep into the rain forest.

Finally the Song left him.

'Here,' it said. 'Wait here.'

Then it had faded, whispering wraith-like through the trees, leaving Kimathi standing in silence.

As the Song left him reality returned. He found

himself in a cool clearing, encircled and overhung with the tangled branches and aerial roots of ancient trees. It was dim and oppressive and dripping with moisture. The air was chill and he shivered as the perspiration cooled on his body. He pulled the cape of skin around him and hunched down against a tree. He leaned the slender spear against the trunk but kept his hand poised at the shaft, ready and alert. Now that the Song was gone he was afraid and uncertain.

'Wait,' the Song had said.

Wait for what?

His eyes searched anxiously around the clearing.

What was he to do now?

He tried to read the forest with his eyes and ears and mind. Tried to see if the forest would tell him what he must do. As his breathing slowed he began to hear, out beyond the deep quiet of the clearing, the soft whirrs of invisible wings as sunbirds sewed threads of sound through the high branches, distant crashings as monkeys rattled through tree tops, and far off rifle-cracks of trees bulldozed to the ground by elephant.

But the Song stayed silent.

And in the clearing the minutes padded, with long slow steps, through the heavy afternoon.

He became drowsy. The great forest peace began to wash away his fear and his eyes began to droop. The light seeping down from the roof of branches began to fade to twilight. Here and there a blade of grass hissed, a leaf rustled, a droplet of water tapped to the ground. Kimathi's hand slipped from the spear and his head gradually nodded on to his chest.

Momentarily he started as he thought he heard a soft rustling, a swishing of undergrowth, just beyond the limits of sight. He flicked his eyes towards it, but the gloom was deepening and he could see nothing in the gathering velvet shadows. He decided that he had imagined it.

His eyes closed again.

He slept.

He was no longer in the forest but lying, belly-down, crouched in the long grass of the plain. It was night and a high, silver moon had stripped the colour from the world.

Raising his head slightly above the grass he swept a quick, appraising glance around, with the urgency of hunger, of blood-lust.

Then he sank down again and lay looking at the picture in his mind, analysing the shapes, assessing.

Away to the right, close to the water-hole, a small group of zebra stood motionless and silent. Behind them, like black, hunched boulders against the grey rock of a kopje, a troop of baboons shuffled and grumbled themselves into positions for the night. To the left, giraffe, dwarfing the mushrooms of the thorn trees, slept in silent silhouette in the pale moonlight. Beyond them a lone hyena, still as a gravestone, stood hypnotized by the moon.

African night. Serengeti stillness.

Nothing moving but the leopard, who kills by dark.

He made his decision and began to slide forward. Slowly, slowly. So stealthily that the grass he parted seemed not to move. Then, when he judged that the black shadow-pools of the trees would conceal him, he rose and began to pad silently round in an arc which would bring him to the foot of the kopje, within a few feet of the somnolent, gently grunting baboons.

His mouth began to salivate as he went, his throat aching for the warm blood of the kill. His eyes burned through the night air, yellow and hunger-filled, fixing his prey, pinning it to the rock, willing it to be still until his jaws closed upon it. His soft paws continued their steady pad, soundless and infinitely delicate on the yielding Serengeti earth. His body seemed built of air, weightless, floating over the ground, silent as water, smooth as oil.

And then, with a soft snarl, he was up and running, hurtling over the last yards to the kopje. The startled zebras whirled away, flickering and dancing, their hooves a hollow drum-roll as he slid past them.

The baboons woke instantly. Jumping to their feet, they began to bark and snarl, simultaneously terror-ized and challenging, their huge, dog-like heads jer-king from side to side trying to see where the danger came from. Then they fled in fifty directions, nimble and swift, leaping from rock to rock up the kopje or down on to the plain, a chattering, gibbering, bounding, lolloping confetti of animals cast on to the wind by a giant, cruel hand.

He pin-pointed one, a young female slower to move than the rest, weighed down by a cub clinging to her back. He went for her, hurling himself up the rocks after her in a spitting torrent of fur and flesh until with one, last, curving bound, he thudded heavily on to her back and sank his teeth into her neck. She fell heavily, paralysed with fear. The cub twisted out from under them and scurried away, yelping, into the darkness. He closed his jaws tighter, encircling her neck, choking off her life-giving air. Blood began to seep into his mouth, slaking the terrible thirst, calming the hunger.

Then, with his victory flowing slowly into his mouth, it was snatched away from him.

Thumping heavily from rock to rock, bellowing great barks of outrage and fury, red eyes burning with challenge, the huge male patriarch and protector of the troop smashed down on him with a force that knocked the wind from him. His jaws involuntarily released their grip on his prey as he gasped for air. The female instantly leaped up and scuttled away through the rocks, shrieking her pain and humiliation as she went.

The old male hurled himself at him again, doghead jaws wide, snapping and grunting.

Still dazed from the first onslaught he tried to protect himself by sitting back on his hind legs and lashing out at the snarling head with his front paws. The baboon was too quick for him. Rolling deftly to one side it easily avoided the raking claws, came up out of the roll, sank its great incisors deeply into its adversary's shoulder and, with a quick flick of its powerful head and shoulders, flung him to one side, like a petulant child hurling a rag doll into a corner. That done, it turned and, whooping with triumph, disappeared into the night.

The fall had knocked the wind out of him again and he lay for a long while gasping sulkily. Gradually his breathing quietened and the pain from his shoulder receded.

The kopje and the plains had quietened too. The baboons had gone; the zebra and giraffe had drummed and lolloped away across the night plain; the lone hyena had gone to bay at another moon.

He rolled carefully to his feet and began to climb to the crest of the kopje. His front paw dragged a little with the wound to his shoulder, but the pain was slight and he ignored it. But he could not ignore his hunger, his thirst for blood. Could not ignore his failure.

He stood finally at the top of the kopje staring out over the night plains. They were empty. Everything had gone to hide. He would hunt no more that night. His tail swung angrily from side to side and he gave out his disappointment in a long, rasping series of barks which sawed out through the night air of Serengeti, bouncing in dying echoes across the flat grasslands.

At first Kimathi did not remember the dream.

The dawn birds woke him with their shrill, clear bells ringing in the new day and he lay quietly for a while, marvelling at how deeply he had slept in this unfamiliar place. The forest was heavy with dawn dew and it pattered down from the trees like gentle rainfall around and upon him. He was very cold again, the coldness of dank air and sleep. As he had tossed and turned during the night the warm leopard-skin cape had slipped away from his shoulders. It lay crumpled beside him.

He reached out and pulled it towards him, and as he did so a flash of red caught his eye.

Sitting up he opened out the skin to examine it.

In the right shoulder were two neat holes. Fresh blood, still wet, circled them.

Then he remembered the dream.

And as he remembered he gave a single cry of shock. A single, harsh, rasping cry which was answered by a chatter and crash of startled monkeys.

Then silence.

six

Alan's father had made light of the dead chicken and the roughly scrawled word.

'Nothing to do with us,' he had said. 'Whatever this thing is that's going on, it's between them. It's no good us trying to fathom it. There's things go on out there that have their roots way back; tribal hatreds, long-remembered wars, land disputes from years back, generations back even. It's their problem, not ours. Forget it.'

But his actions belied his words. A couple of days later Alan awoke to the sound of hacksaws rasping on metal and the scream of electric drills shattering the calm morning air.

He emerged to a house swarming with workmen.

'What in heaven's name's going on?' he enquired anxiously as he joined his parents for breakfast on the veranda.

'Don't worry, dear, it's just a precaution, that's all. Everyone has security grilles on their windows down in Moshi and no one thinks anything of it. Your father has just decided to catch up with the times, that's all.'

She smiled a smile of reassurance, but it was not too convincing.

'Dad, Moshi's different, you know that. All the thieves and vagabonds gather in the towns. We've never had any trouble up here. Half the time we don't even remember to lock our doors and still we never have things stolen. Now, all of a sudden, we're going to live inside a wrought-iron cage and you say "forget it". You're treating me like a child. If you suspect something dangerous is going to happen, tell me. I'm eighteen, for goodness' sake.'

But his father wouldn't be drawn.

'Precaution,' he repeated. 'There's no one around here would mean us any harm, I'm sure. But if something is going to blow up we might just, accidentally, get caught up in it. I don't have the first idea what's happening, but I've seen tribal fights before and I'm not taking any chances. If they want to start waving knives about and firing guns at each other that's their affair. Our only danger, and it's a small one, is that they might get so excited they won't know who they're waving their knives at, friend or foe. That's what the grilles are for. Precaution.'

Alan sighed.

'OK,' he said, more to humour his father than anything else.

'So, put it out of your mind. Your mother and I have to go down to Moshi now to pay all these bills. Kimathi should be doing this but he seems to have disappeared from the face of the earth. It's days since he last came to work.'

'I know,' Alan said. 'He's not been to see me since I came back. It's very puzzling.'

'That's Africa,' his father replied, smiling wryly.

'Puzzling.' He rose, gathered up a bundle of papers from the table and set off across the garden to where the Land-Rover was parked.

'See you later,' he called as he went.

Alan's mother paused for a moment on the veranda steps as she followed him.

'It's all right, dear, really. Your father knows what he's doing, I'm sure. These people are our friends.'

She smiled again at her son, then turned, hurried across the garden and climbed into the Land-Rover.

'We'll be back some time this afternoon,' she called, as the big machine began to crunch down the drive.

As the engine noise faded Alan sat quietly gathering his thoughts. His parents had been no reassurance and Alan shook his head worriedly.

He had been going to tackle his father about the other thing that was disturbing him but, at the last second, had lost his nerve. There was something much more worrying than the ugly grilles appearing at the windows, or the heavy wrought-iron gate at the entrance to the corridor which led to their bedrooms.

The missing gun frightened him more than any of these things.

For as long as he could remember the long hunting-rifles had stood, gathering dust, in their securely locked case on the living-room wall. Only once in his lifetime had he seen one used when, years ago, a stumbling glazed-eyed dog, rabid and terrifyingly insane, had wandered into the garden. His father had dispatched it, cleanly and without emotion, and the gun had joined its companions for another decade of inaction.

Now there was a gaping, disturbing space in the rack, as persistently obvious as a missing tooth, as nagging to the mind as toothache.

Iron bars might well be a sensible precaution in a country where poverty has defeated respect for other people's property, but a gun is more than a precaution. A gun is an intention.

A gun standing in readiness by your father's bed is a potent premonition.

The crashings and sawings from inside the house were beginning to get on Alan's nerves.

He decided to go and find Njombo to see if he could discover more from him than he could from his father. Stepping over the piles of iron bars, he wandered through the house to the kitchen.

Njombo was sitting quietly at the big wooden table in the centre of the room, peeling vegetables for dinner. Alan watched him for a moment from the doorway. Njombo continued his task, his hands, knuckles swollen with arthritis, painfully chipping the skins from potatoes with a small knife. He was unaware that he was being watched.

Surely, Alan thought, his father could not be right? Whatever was happening, Njombo would never lie to them. This small, dark figure was part of the family; had been part of Alan's life for ever, for as long as he had memory. Always there, always the same, dependable and changeless, as warm and comforting and eternal in his presence as the house itself with its friendly creaks and calm safety. Those hands were the same hands that had lifted him as a child or dried his tears when he fell. The lined face was the same gentle, considerate face which had smiled upon him over the years. This man, surely, could not deceive them, could not have changed.

Alan cleared his throat to warn the man that he was there.

Njombo turned his head sharply, startled at the sound. He had been deeply lost in thought. His eyes caught Alan's for a second and a flicker of warmth passed over them. But he averted them quickly; too quickly.

'Bwana Alan,' he said. 'Habari? How are you?'

'Mzuri,' Alan replied. 'I'm fine. I'm sorry, Njombo, I didn't mean to startle you.'

'It is nothing, bwana. I was journeying far away in my thoughts.'

'Where were you?'

'I was here, bwana, but far away in the past. I was hearing two little boys shouting as they ran in the garden.'

He looked directly at Alan again. His eyes were very sad as he spoke.

'But now they are gone again.'

'I'm still here,' Alan said, gently. 'I'm still the little boy you hear. But where is the other boy? Where is Kimathi? I have been home a week and he has not once been to the house since I came back.'

'I know, bwana, and my heart cries to see it.'

'What's happening, Njombo? Something's wrong, we all feel it. What's going on?'

'Oh, bwana, you must not ask, for I can give no answer.'

'Njombo, I must ask. We are all worried. Why does my father suddenly decide we need to live in a prison cell? Why does Kimathi avoid me and no longer come to work? Have we done something to make everybody angry with us?'

Njombo's eyes turned from sadness to hurt.

'No, bwana, no one is angry with you; you must not think that. What is happening is happening to the people from elsewhere. Not from you.'

He rose and hobbled quickly to the door. He put his head out, scanned around the garden, then, satisfied that he would not be overheard, returned.

'Bwana Alan, you must go away. Tell your father that he must take you and your mother away.'

His voice was quietly urgent now, his face creased with earnest concern.

Alan was shocked.

'Go away? Njombo, this is our home. How can we go away? Where will we go?'

'Please, bwana, go to Moshi. Stay in the town until this thing has passed. It will not be long. One week. Two. Then it will be over. When you return things will be as before.'

'But why Njombo?' Alan's voice quavered with alarm now. 'You must tell me why.'

'I cannot, bwana.' He looked over his shoulder anxiously, making sure no one else was around. 'Only this can I tell you. You are here at a bad time, a time of magic. It is a time very important to us. A time for the black man, not the white. Please, bwana, tell your father you must go. I have told you too much already. Go.'

'Njombo, my father will never go away from here. Who would supervise the work if he went?'

'The work will stop soon, bwana. Already the people are restless, waiting for a sign. The work will stop. They must do other things.'

Alan was silent for a long moment, stunned and afraid by what he was hearing. His father had been right, things were changed, terribly changed, and Njombo was part of it. Njombo knew what was happening and was afraid for them. This man, who had only good in his heart, was warning them that there was danger here.

'And Kimathi?' he asked of the old man. 'What of Kimathi?'

'He has gone to the mountain,' answered Njombo, 'to bring us the sign. We depend on him now.'

He looked gently at Alan, knowing that what he said next would be deeply disturbing to the boy.

'Bwana, this you must know. The Kimathi you knew is no more. The boy is gone. Now the man must tread another path.'

Alan stared at him in disbelief.

'It is true, bwana. The path he treads is a path of danger, for him and for all of us. You must not try to follow his path. Forget Kimathi now, your days together are finished. What he does now he must do, he cannot escape it. None of the Chagga can escape it. But you can. Go. Come back when it is over.'

He turned away and sat down once more at the table.

'That is all, bwana Alan,' he said. 'My heart hurts for you, but now I say no more.'

And he took up his knife and returned to the vegetables with a finality that could not be misunderstood. The conversation was over. He would give no more.

Alan's brain was whirling as he turned away from the kitchen and began to wander back through the house to the veranda. He was deeply shocked. Suddenly everything felt unreal to him. Njombo's words had shattered his security. How could he be in danger here? This was his home. Africa was his home. Home was the place you ran to when everything else was crumbling.

And he was as much a part of Africa as Kimathi and Njombo. Though his skin was white he was African nevertheless. Njombo's words, 'A time for the black man, not the white', had shocked him. He had believed himself to be something he apparently was not. In the eyes of the black African he was just 'a white man'. Even, it seemed, in Njombo's eyes. Perhaps even in Kimathi's too.

He slumped into a chair and tried to shut out his dismay. What should he do? It would be no use telling his father what Njombo had said. Alan knew his father well enough to know that he would not leave this house for a day, let alone two weeks. He would fly into a temper, start shouting at everyone and demanding to know what was going on and make things worse than ever.

No, if there was danger they would simply have to stay and face it; and he, Alan, would have to try and stay one step ahead of it; keep his eyes and ears and mind open; try to read people without them knowing it; try to piece events together and see where they led.

He looked out across the forest slopes. Their soothing green was hung with a soft smoke of white mist as the morning sun began to dry out the night dew. The cloud base hanging on the mountain had risen so that the long saddle between Mawenzi and Kibo was in view for the first time since his return.

This too, this vast colossus thrusting up from the plains of Africa to pierce the sky three miles above his head, was home. He had climbed upon this mountain with Kimathi a thousand times; sat at the huge, black-banded face they called Zebra Rocks and watched the storms fling bright splodges of snow on to the crumbling spires of Mawenzi as though a giant paintbrush splattered them with white; climbed with him high on to the snow-covered dome of Kibo itself, to Uhuru Peak, to the roof of all Africa, where the air was so thin you gasped and retched with every movement.

And now Njombo was telling him that these days were over; that this place was no longer his place; that the friendship of a lifetime could evaporate, without word, in a week.

How could this be true?

It couldn't. Alan knew that it couldn't be true.

Whatever Kimathi was doing, whatever he had to do, nothing could destroy the bond they had between them. A bond built, cemented from the very earliest days of childhood could not just vanish like this, without trace.

Kimathi was the key to this frightening and daunting puzzle, Alan decided. Whatever the danger was that Njombo could see but would not reveal, Kimathi would know it too. And no danger could ever come to Alan from Kimathi, of that he was certain.

So, that was it. He had to find him. Kimathi would tell him what was happening and what to do.

'A time of magic,' Njombo had said. 'A time for the black man, not the white.'

Well, there were things stronger than magic. Stronger than race or colour or culture.

Friendship and trust were stronger than all these things; and, if he could find Kimathi, together they would prove it.

Alan stood and stared up at the mountain, feeling more confident now. If Kimathi was there then he would be able to find him. He would be near the familiar places, the places they had visited together.

Even if it took days Alan would find him.

He decided to go immediately. In three hours he could be at the Mandara Huts where the climbers and porters would be gathered. Perhaps there someone would have seen Kimathi.

He turned to go back into the house to make his preparations. He would need a rucksack, some food and his sleeping-bag.

As he passed through the french windows into the living room he paused as something caught his attention.

From somewhere high on the forest slopes he had

heard a sound, faint but unmistakeable, floating down on the heavy morning dampness. The single, harsh, rasping cough of a leopard, followed by an answering chatter and crash of startled monkeys.

Then the forest became silent again.

He dismissed it and stepped into the house.

seven

Commander Sebastian Makayowe was a very large man.

His six-foot-six, twenty-stone frame was massively resplendent in his starched, royal-blue uniform. Gold-braided, bemedalled, crowned with his peaked commander's cap, he bore an uncanny resemblance to that vicious, vengeful madman of Uganda, Idi Amin.

He relished the likeness, cultivated it even, for its power to strike terror into the hearts of the steady stream of criminals who found their nefarious paths diverted through the doors of Moshi Police Station. Those unfortunates who did find themselves inside would discover that the commander's temper, like Amin's, was as massive and as daunting as his frame. And on Monday mornings, as the weekend's scum of muggers, knifers, house-breakers, car-thieves, drunks, cattle-rustlers and murderers floated to the surface of his town, it was at its worst.

He could hear the noise as soon as he switched off the engine of the police Landcruiser. He sighed irritably. Moshi Police Station at nine o'clock on a Monday morning was a depressing place.

As he walked down the path a great cacophonous

babble was rising from the building. Inside, his men would be desperately trying to beat and bludgeon some order into the criminal rabble they had picked off the seething, weekend streets. He could hear the shouted protestations as heads were cuffed or backsides kicked by weary, irascible constables, mingled with the angry demands for attention from complainants whose cows were missing, houses ransacked or husbands knifed in bar fights.

Here was all the criminal life that swilled its way around this dirty, crumbling African town, trailing destruction, dismay and death in its wake.

A fair imitation of hell, thought Makayowe for the hundredth time.

But on Monday mornings the commander was a fair imitation of the devil, as those inside were soon to find out.

He stopped for a second as he reached the door, then, drawing himself up, he booted it open. His polished toe-cap thudded, surely and accurately, into the splintered depression made by thousands of previous ill-tempered bootings. The door crashed back on to the inner wall with a violence which threatened to wrench it from its hinges. The noise of the crash and the sudden flood of light into the interior quietened the deafening babble to a respectful hum as a hundred anxious heads turned.

The light dimmed as the huge bulk of the commander rolled forward to fill the doorway.

He surveyed the swirling scene.

His eyes narrowed and the veins in his neck bulged. A respectful hum was not respect enough when he, Commander Sebastian Makayowe, entered a room. Respect was silence. Nothing else would do.

'Silence,' he hissed, through clenched teeth. 'You snakes, you dung-beetles. Silence.'

The noise faded rapidly.

Satisfied, he walked slowly into the room, eyes flickering disdainfully around the now wary throng of detainees. The ones who had been here before averted their faces or scurried into hiding behind others, for they knew the quiet anger of this man, recognized the gently bubbling volcano of rage which could surface, at any capricious moment, in an eruption of flying fists and boots, and bellowed outrage that they had broken his laws.

HIS laws. Not the country's. In Moshi there was Tanzanian law and Makayowe's law.

And Makayowe's law was the more feared.

Now the room was completely silent and heavy with expectation.

A drunk, emerging from a crippling hangover and nursing a seeping knife-wound to the arm, moaned gently in private agony on a bench against the wall. With a violence made even more cruel by its casualness, Makayowe reached out as he passed, grasped the man's tightly bunched curls in a huge, gorilla-haired hand and smashed his head against the wall. There was a sickening, hollow crack which brought a gasp from even the hardest of the criminals. The drunk gave a single, strangled moan, slid to the floor and was still.

The commander continued across the room to the

desk where his sergeant, rigidly at attention, saluted him with trembling hand.

Makayowe turned and surveyed the now cringing crowd.

'So,' he hissed, 'snakes.'

His measured tones were heavy with menace.

'This is what you will do. You will make two lines here, to this desk. You will remain silent until you are asked to speak. Then, when you are asked, you will tell your miserable stories to my sergeant and my constables. You will tell them that you did not do it! That the cow was really yours! That you meant to return the car! That when the man was killed with the machete you were in another part of the town! And you will tell us that we have arrested the wrong man.'

A benign, fatherly smile had appeared gradually on his face as he spoke. Now he spread his arms expansively as though he were about to announce a general pardon and tell everyone that they could go home. The crowd waited for the glad announcement.

'Then,' Makayowe continued, happily, 'when we have listened to your stories – we will lock you up. We will ask you again tomorrow. And the next day. And the next. For you will have lied. And we will know you have lied. Soon – in a day or two – you will tell the truth. We will – persuade – you to tell the truth.'

He drew out the word 'persuade' so that it hissed around the room like a snake on the point of striking. No one in the room could doubt that the persuasion would be short, brutal and implacably effective.

'And that,' said Commander Makayowe as he turned and strolled towards the corridor leading to his office, 'is that.'

He put the detainees out of his mind. This was just another Monday morning in an endless succession of Monday mornings. Just another clean-up of the human sewage which leaked constantly into his beloved town. Even as this batch was being sanitized, flushed away, so another batch would be starting to build, inexorable as the days followed the days.

And indeed, for this particular Monday morning, that would have been that, if it had not been for the man waiting patiently in the commander's office. The man who had pretended to his son that his journey down to Moshi was to pay bills, but who had a much more urgent purpose.

John Edwards waited in Commander Makayowe's office.

eight

On the hour-long drive from Marangu down to Moshi John Edwards had had time to think.

Despite all his protestations of ignorance about what was happening, and despite all his calm reassurances to his family that they would not be involved, he knew more than he was admitting. And because he had seen something like this before, when he was Alan's age, the knowledge struck fear into him. He was pretty sure that he could not deal with this alone. For this he would need the help of his old friend Sebastian Makayowe.

He had had his suspicions right from the beginning when the workers became unpredictable and surly. The headless chicken suspended on his property and the horrifying, blood-daubed word had confirmed them. He had been singled out. His property marked.

The signs were the same as he remembered them as a boy in Kenya. The darkness was beginning again, as it had in his father's generation, and the generation before that and, for all he knew, for countless other generations. The darkness of violence and tribal magic which had made the first white men speak of 'darkest Africa'. A darkness not of the land itself, of impenetrable jungle or unexplored vastnesses, but the darkness in the hearts of men. That was what they had meant.

Now it was here again. The word CHUI scrawled on the wall could mean only one thing. The Leopard Cult was rising in this generation just as it had in the last. The tribes were demanding blood as they had in the 1950s.

On that occasion the white man had explained it as best he could. It was all political, he said. Kenya had tired of slavery; had tired of the white man being in control; had wanted its independence.

'When the white man came,' Kenyatta had said, 'he had the Bible and we had the land. He taught us to close our eyes and pray. When we opened our eyes we had the Bible and he had the land.'

They had wanted their land back and the Mau Mau terror had been a means of achieving that end, the raids on isolated settlers' farms a well-organized campaign of harassment.

The murders of white families had been regrettable of course, but the Mau Mau had simply been drawing attention to their cause. And not many whites had been killed after all. In all the years of the Mau Mau campaign more whites had been killed in accidents on the pot-holed, red-dust roads than had died at the hands of the terrorists.

So it had been a great storm in a very small teacup, hadn't it? The uprising had been crushed, Kenya had gained its independence, everything had gone quiet, and now it was all forgiven and forgotten and would never happen again.

That was what the white man believed.

And, as always, the Africans let the white man believe what he wanted to believe. Told him what he wanted to hear.

But John Edwards's bones had told him something different at the time and they were telling him something different now. For there had been stories which had told a different tale. Stories which hinted at things beneath the surface; things incredible but which gained credibility with repetition; things magic, which the wordly-wise dismissed as fantasy but which were never explained.

He recalled the story of the young British lieutenant who surprised a Mau Mau attack on a remote settler's farm. As the assailants had scattered under his fire he had singled out, so the story went, one leopard-skin-clad Kikuyu and coolly slammed three bullets into his chest. Mortally wounded, the man had escaped into the bush. The lieutenant had tracked him for four miles, following the bright splashes of blood; tracked him with infinite care. And finally he had caught up with him. Under the enervating heat of an African noon, in the silence of the Maasai Mara plain he had found him, dead, at the foot of an acacia. The vivid blood-trail had been clear and unmistakeable, without break, without any deviation. It had led directly to the body.

But the body the lieutenant found had not been that of a Kikuyu. It had been the body of a full-grown male leopard. Eyes glazed in death, mouth open in a dying gasp, the remaining blood still draining from the three clean, clear bullet holes in its chest.

A full-grown male leopard.

Everyone had dismissed the story as fantasy, of course. The young lieutenant had had too much sun, that was the verdict. African sun can do that, everyone agreed. 'Everyone' meaning 'everyone white'.

No African, John Edwards was thinking to himself as he sat waiting in Commander Makayowe's office, would be so ready to dismiss the story. And now it had returned to haunt him.

His musings were shattered as the office door crashed open and the battleship bulk of the commander sailed in.

His face beamed.

'Bwana John,' he bellowed happily, 'karibu. Welcome.'

They shook hands.

'Sebastian, forgive me for disturbing you on a Monday morning, but I have a problem.'

'Of course,' said the commander, crashing down into his chair, 'or you would not be here. No one comes to see Sebastian Makayowe unless they have a problem.'

He chuckled.

'And,' he added, 'as everyone knows, there is no problem that Sebastian Makayowe cannot solve.'

He spread his hands enquiringly.

'So,' he demanded. 'Tell me.'

Twenty minutes later a much happier John Edwards left through the front door of Moshi Police Station and climbed into his Land-Rover. He had desperately needed reassurance, and Makayowe had delivered it.

'Trouble-makers,' Makayowe had shouted. 'Miserable, creeping dung-beetles of trouble-makers who will wish they had not been born. Go about your business and forget them, bwana John. They are less than ants and I will crush them. Tomorrow my men will come to Marangu. We will find out who is doing this thing. We will catch them and we will lock them up. Forget them. Now they are mine.'

And the huge, all-encompassing confidence of the man had lifted the burden of fear from John Edwards's shoulders and sent him back to the quiet slopes of Marangu ensured of the safety of his farm, of his wife and son, and of himself, confident now that the solid wall of Commander Makayowe and his men stood between them and the gathering dangers.

But as the office door had closed and Sebastian Makayowe was left alone the smile of farewell had faded from his face. The face he had presented to John Edwards was the face of Makayowe the policeman. But Commander Makayowe was something else too.

He was an African.

And though he would do everything in his power to uphold the law, to protect the lives of this quiet, likeable white man and his family, there was a small voice whispering in his heart.

The ancient voice of his African, tribal blood was saying, over and over:

'There is no escape. There is no escape. There is no . . .'

nine

Kimathi, alone in the silent forest clearing, did not know what to do.

He had waited all day for the Song to begin again, at any moment expecting the soft hum from the mountain to stir in his blood. Without the Song he was lost, purposeless and without confidence. Its absence was an ache, like the ache of loneliness

And as the hours had trickled quietly away he had become afraid that the Song would not return at all.

The story had not prepared him for this. He knew what his part in it was; to learn the Song, to run with the Leopard Spirit, to kill with the Leopard. That had always been his destiny and the Chagga tribe depended on him to fulfil it. Even now, down at the village, people would be glancing anxiously at the Tree of Man, waiting for the leopard-head flowers to appear, the sign that for another generation the tribe would be safe, would survive.

But the flowers would not appear unless Kimathi succeeded, proved himself fit. And the story had not told him how he should do that.

Perhaps he had failed already.

'Run as the Leopard and hear its Song,

Kill as the Leopard and be the Song,' WaChui had said.

He had done as he had been bidden, he was sure of that. He had followed the Song where it had led him, had run in the night grass of Serengeti and hunted on the dream-plain.

But he had not killed. Was that why the Song had not returned?

Surely, he thought, he could not be expected to learn his part in this strange magic-play so quickly. The play was performed only once in the lifetime of a man, directed by a force as old as the mountain. Surely the force which had chosen him, marked him, would give him time to learn his part in things.

He looked again and again at the leopard pelt lying on the grass beside him. The blood had dried to a deep, russet-brown. The two neat holes in the centres of the stains glared at him like the black, accusing pupils of disappointed eyes. He was disturbed by the implicit judgement of him that they bore, and by the tangible, baffling testament that his life was now sewn with a thread of magic, beyond comprehension and entirely beyond his control.

What had happened last night, *really* happened on the night-plain of Serengeti?

Had he run with the leopard in a Song-induced dream? Had it been a memory of an act long past but stored, carried through the years, in the supple membrane of the long-dead leopard pelt he wore? A memory with the power to reactivate the cold hatred which flows through the veins of this most vicious and vengeful of animals, bringing its spirit to its soft feet again to pad the night in silent dream?

Or was it more than that?

Had the body that reoccupied this skin, that had endowed it once again with muscles of steel and silk and speed and silence, been a leopard's body or his body?

Had he watched the leopard, or was he the leopard?

He did not know, and was afraid to know.

Afraid that the Song would not return, and afraid that it would, he waited.

Alan packed a rucksack with his sleeping-bag, his down-filled anorak and some food. Then, just before three o'clock, he left.

He had expected his mother and father to be back by then but they weren't. He couldn't wait any longer if he was to reach Mandara Huts by dark so he left them a note to tell them what he was doing.

He made his way up the short path through the eucalyptus trees at the back of the house and on to the coffee slopes. The workers were still there, dotted about among the low, green bushes, painstakingly picking off the coffee berries and filling their cane baskets. The men's brightly coloured shirts and the women's vivid kangas stood out against the dull green of the lines of bushes. The sun was very hot still and a heavy, lethargic quiet hung over the day.

Alan smiled and called out greetings as he passed. As always everyone replied. Perhaps it was only his imagination, his uneasiness caused by Njombo's words, but today the replies seemed not so warm.

He had the feeling that the smiles faded the moment he went by.

At the top of the slopes he passed through the cluster of roasting-sheds. The big, round pans inside the sheds were rotating gently over the fires and the pungent smell of roasting coffee filled the air. He glanced into the sheds as he passed but the men had already left. Alan smiled. They weren't supposed to leave until four o'clock, but no doubt word had reached them that 'Boss John' had gone to Moshi and they had taken advantage of the knowledge.

On the other side of the sheds a narrow path led through the forest for about a hundred yards. At the end of it Alan emerged on to the wide climbers' track which led up to Mandara. He stopped for a moment, tilting his head back to trace the long, upward path of the track. Then he pulled the belt-strap of his rucksack tightly around his waist to ease the pull on his shoulders and started the ascent.

At first climbing felt awkward and he had to concentrate to find his rhythm; but soon he had fallen into the steady, energy-saving, mountaineer's plod which would take him effortlessly up the steep ascent.

Two hours later, he passed within two hundred yards of where his friend Kimathi sat, confused and afraid, in a silent forest clearing.

In the late afternoon the men fetched the drums from the old man's cave and set them ready at the far end of the clearing.

In the centre of the circle of huts they built a huge mound of wood for the fire.

Then they went into their huts to prepare themselves. Inside, they removed their clothes, the hated white man's uniform of shirts and shorts. They rolled them neatly and tied them in bundles. Later they would burn them, the symbols of their subjection, of their taming by another race, vanishing into smoke. In their place they put on the ancient loin-cloths of beaten mulberry bark which had been handed down from father to son through all the generations of their tribe.

The women brought the gourds of grease and, in the dim light of the huts, oiled the skins of their men until they shone like polished ebony. Then they painted them, dabbing neat circles of deep, yellow-ochre on to their bodies, arms and legs as though they covered them with golden, staring eyes.

The men painted their faces themselves, as they had been taught how to do, with swathes of yellow across their foreheads and cheeks and heavy yellow circles around their eyes.

Then, as darkness began to fall, they emerged one by one from their huts.

When it was fully dark they lit the fire. As it crackled and winked sparks up into the sky they threw their bundles of clothes on to the flames and freed themselves from the chains the flimsy fabric represented.

Freed themselves to be again what they were. Chagga warriors.

They sat, arranging themselves in a circle around the clearing, the great Ntenga drum at one end.

And then they waited. Waited for the Watcher of the Tree.

Waited for their time to come.

ten

Alan arrived at the Mandara Huts just as darkness was falling.

As always the place was swarming with climbers, and as always they were loud, enthusiastic and high-spirited, fooled by how easy they had found the first day's climb to be.

Alan smiled to himself. He had seen it all before many times.

The first day is easy. A gently rising path through the rain forest with shady glades for rest and cool streams to ease burning throats and sweating bodies. A slow, calm walk from Marangu Gate at seven thousand feet to Mandara Huts at eleven and a half.

'A piece of cake,' he heard a loud Australian say.

They wouldn't be so loud and confident at the next huts, Alan reflected. By the time they reached Horombo, at the end of the second day, their voices would be more subdued, more serious. And, now and then, you would be able to catch a flash of anxiety passing across their eyes as they glanced fitfully up towards Kibo. By Horombo they would be realizing that Kilima Njaro had deceived them, had lulled them into under-estimating it with the soft benignity of its lower slopes.

Fifteen minutes after leaving Mandara Huts these confident climbers would find themselves abruptly stepping out of the tree-line into a harsher landscape. A landscape of endless, scorching moorland where there was no escape from the enervating brilliance and dehydrating blast of the sun. A strange landscape where lobelia and groundsel grew beyond the height of a man, and where, as they battled over the crest of one hard-won slope their hearts would sink as they were confronted with another. And another. And another. Hour after hour.

And if they won through that day and retained their optimism then Kilima Njaro still had plenty of tricks up its sleeve.

The third day would bring the Saddle, an immense and lifeless corridor of black, volcanic dust which would draw in the heat of the sun and breathe it back again through the soles of their feet and the pores of their skin until they would feel they were walking in the embers of a fire.

And, all the time, as they rose from Horombo to Kibo Hut, the air would be getting thinner, and thinner, until their every move would bring their hearts thudding into their throats and their lungs would cry out in pain.

By Kibo Hut they would all be very quiet, their confidence as thin as the atmosphere.

For this is Kilima Njaro's real deception. It is not an African mountain at all. It is an Himalayan mountain, cruelly dropped in the wrong place. A mountain pretending to be benevolent, drawing the unwary ever upwards, but guarding its final summits with a fierce energy of sweeping blizzards, debilitating silences and the draining insubstantiality of its fragile air.

The climbers, good-naturedly roistering into the quiet evening at Mandara, had all this to find out. And Alan, of course, was not going to dash any hopes by telling them that half of them wouldn't get to the summit at all. They would find their limitations, quite literally their 'level', soon enough, when altitude sickness, weariness, or just the great, fearful immensity of the place dispirited them, dismayed them and, finally, drove them down.

But for the moment Alan was glad of their company, his uneasy mind reassured by their humour and carefree confidence.

He made his way to the central hut where everyone would be gathering to eat. A few Tilley lamps were hissing amiably from inside the big, A-shaped wooden building and a clear, white light spilled welcomingly from the doorway out on to the veranda and the wooden steps. The sweet fragrance of woodsmoke hung on the air. The guides and porters were busy at the rear of the hut cooking dinner in huge, blackened pots over open fires and murmuring quietly amongst themselves.

Alan left his rucksack at the foot of the steps and made his way round to them.

'Jambo. Habari?'

'Jambo, bwana. Mzuri. Mzuri sana. Karibu.'

One of the guides stepped forward out of the shadows.

'Ah, Bwana Alan. Welcome. You are home. We have missed you on the mountain.'

'Ruichi. I am glad to see you. Yes, I have been away. In England. But now I am home. How are you?'

'I'm fine, bwana. Fine.'

He dipped a chipped enamel mug into a large black pot of simmering tea and handed it to Alan.

'Here, bwana. Chai.'

'Asante, Ruichi.'

Alan took the tea and cupped his hands around the mug. The dank, early evening chill was beginning to seep in from the wet forests and the scalding drink was welcome. He walked over to one of the fires and sat down beside it. Ruichi joined him.

'Who is with you, bwana?'

'No one, Ruichi. I came up by myself. I didn't leave the farm until three o'clock. I waited for my father to come home but it got too late so I left him a note instead, saying where I was.'

'And why do you climb alone, bwana? It is not good to climb alone, even for you.'

'I know, Ruichi, but I have no choice. I have not come just to climb the mountain. I am looking for Kimathi.'

Ruichi grinned. 'Ah, Kimathi. So Kimathi is lost?'

'No, Ruichi, he is not lost. I am not making a joke. I am serious. This is serious. There is some sort of trouble in Kimathi's village and his father, old Njombo, says Kimathi is up here. There seems to be some sort of danger. Kimathi has stopped coming to work and avoids me. I have to find him and find out what's going on. Do you know what's happening? Have you seen him?'

'No, bwana, to both questions. Like you I have only come up today. Perhaps these others may know something. Some are coming down from the tops. Perhaps they will have seen him.'

He turned and called out his query to the men hunched over the cooking pots or walking around engaged in their various jobs.

There was much clucking and tutting and discussion, but, in the end, it was only to demonstrate willingness. No one could offer any help or advice. No one had seen Kimathi.

'Never mind,' said Alan. 'It was a slim hope. I don't suppose he'll be anywhere near the climbers' track. Tomorrow I'll make my way up to Horombo, then I'll head off around the snow-line towards the Great Barranco. That's where we often used to go. I'd guess that if he needs to be alone to think then that's where he'll be. No one goes round that way much.'

'Take care, bwana. It is very lonely there. If you have an accident you will be on your own.'

'I know, Ruichi. Thanks. If I'm not down in two or three days you can organize a search party.'

'Yes, bwana.'

Alan stood and handed the mug back to the guide.

'If you see Kimathi you'll tell him I'm looking for him and where I've gone?'

'Sure, bwana. Of course.'

'And thanks for the tea.'

'You are welcome, bwana. Good luck.'

Alan walked back around to the front of the hut, picked up his rucksack and made his way inside. Various groups of climbers were seated around the tables playing cards, drinking or simply discussing the day amongst themselves. Someone had lit a fire in the huge stone fireplace at the far end of the room and it crackled and spat cheerfully. Alan walked over to it, opened his rucksack and staked his claim to a sleeping place beside the fire by unrolling his sleeping-bag on to the floor. Then he went and sat on the steps outside the hut.

Darkness had fallen completely now and, looking down the mountain slopes and out on to the endless plains below, he could see fires beyond number glowing and winking from the villages and settlements as their inhabitants prepared their meals or simply sat the evening away telling stories in the companionable glow. Overhead the vast vault of African sky shimmered with a million, million stars, as though it mimicked the fires, caught them up and multiplied them to an infinity of sky-borne villages.

Alan shuddered a little. Sometimes the hugeness of Africa dismayed him.

'Go to Africa to heal the heart,' they say. But 'humble it' might be nearer. It was easy to feel insignificant, powerless, up here in the face of such size, such immense age and such teeming multitudes of life. Easy to feel that your tiny speck of life was of no importance at all to Africa. That should you disappear Africa would not even notice.

And perhaps he was powerless.

Perhaps Njombo was right.

'Forget Kimathi,' he had said.

The words had been echoing in his mind all day as he journeyed up the path.

'None of us can escape it. Except you.' That was what he had said. 'Except you.'

So, if there was an escape, Alan asked himself yet again, why was he not taking the easy way out? Why was he not at home haranguing his father, persuading him to go away for a time? He knew, secretly, that in spite of all his bluster, his father would have agreed in the end, would finally have placed his son's safety above everything else.

So what was he doing here on the mountain? Why get involved? Why try to change events? Why not just leave things alone and let Africa get on with it?

Well, because he was involved, whether he liked it or not, that's why. Of course they could leave. Nothing could be easier, more simple to arrange. They could go to Nairobi or Mombasa, lounge by a swimming-pool, have a holiday. Wait until the danger was over.

But what would that solve? They had to come home sometime.

And there was the paradox. Would it still be home when they returned to it, or would it, by the very act of leaving it, be something else? 'Home' is not a house, it is something much less tangible. 'Home' is memory, and time past, and the people who have journeyed the days with you. The walls which enclose you are built not of wood or stone but of the lives you have touched and those that have touched you. Run away from home and you run away from the friendly ghosts of time. And by doing so you lose them.

The house *was* Alan and his parents and Njombo and Kimathi. If they allowed events to drive them away then 'home' would be gone for ever, because the years of happiness and friendship, trust and love would be gone for ever. And that was unthinkable.

That was why he was here on the mountain, chasing the chimera that Kimathi had become. For unless he found him, unless they, together, conquered this thing, this 'time of danger', then there was no home anywhere. Then he would truly be insignificant. To Africa, to events, but, most importantly, to himself.

If he lost the small corner of his life that he called home, then he would have lost himself.

He stood up, dropped down the hut steps and walked down the grassy slope to where he could look up at the great, dark bulk of the mountain behind him. The daytime clouds had lifted from the summit and, for the first time since he had returned to Africa, he could see the vast, snow-capped dome of Kibo. It lay silent and silvered by the moon, like a shimmering cloud floating in space, its immense, plunging glaciers flashing starlight like a myriad mirrors. It looked so close he felt he could almost reach up and touch it.

His eyes scanned across from right to left, taking in its bulk, identifying well-known, well-loved contours. Bismarck Towers; Gillman's Point; the great South East Valley; Window Buttress; and The Great Barranco.

And rearing above all, nearly two miles over his

73

head, clear and ghost-white against the night sky, the highest point of all Africa, Uhuru Peak.

His eyes rested long on this place, a place he had trodden many times.

Uhuru.

Named because this high place drew, to a single, ice-bound point, the hopes of all Africa.

Uhuru.

Freedom.

Tomorrow he would be within striking distance of the great ice-fields. He felt sure that he would find Kimathi up there. That was where he would be drawn if he was troubled. To the high lonelinesses of the peaks, where the world was washed clean and purified by the scouring wind. A wind that could cleanse the mind as surely as it cleansed the rocks. There, free from the world, above the world, he would find him.

And there they would solve this problem.

He decided to go back into the hut and get bedded down for the night. If he slept now he could leave about four o'clock in the morning and be at Horombo by eleven. That way he could cross the saddle in the afternoon and be at Kibo Hut, above the snow-line, before dark. Then the next day he would have all day to search for Kimathi.

He began to walk back towards the hut. The ground sloped gently upwards and, as he neared the hut, the big A-frame building loomed gradually higher in front of him, creeping up the floating white apparition of Kibo with each step he took.

Just before the building obscured his view of the

peak he stopped, momentarily entranced by a strange trick of the light.

The moon was shining directly on to the Rebmann Glacier. He could see the great ice-sheet with perfect lucidity.

But that was not what held him. The glacier seemed to be bending the light, angling it away from itself and distilling it into a single, fierce beam directed, with startling intensity, at an area just to the right of Gillman's Point. In turn the ice-walls there bent the light again, redirected it and sent it flashing down the mountain as though someone had switched on a huge, unearthly spotlight.

Alan stood, mesmerized by the strangeness of it, trying to identify where it came from. It seemed to be up beyond Hans Meyer Cave. Somewhere close to Leopard Point.

Then, suddenly, it was gone, switched off abruptly as the moon moved a tiny degree across the sky.

Alan smiled, glad to have seen this new trick of Kilima Njaro. This mountain was full of surprises. Then he walked forward, ascended the steps into the hut and climbed fully clothed into his sleeping-bag.

Just before he pulled the bag up over his head to shut out the light from the lamps, a noise drifted up from somewhere in the forest below them.

'Dear God,' exclaimed an anxious tourist, 'what was that?'

Alan chuckled to himself. 'Only a leopard,' he called. 'There's usually one around here. Don't worry, he won't bother us.'

Then he slept.

eleven

It was nearly midnight before the Watcher arrived in the village.

The fire had burned its course and had settled to a fierce, hot glow. The redness of its heat glinted on the oiled skins of the warriors and the yellow circles on their bodies glowed like a thousand eyes in the night. Profound shadows flitted and jerked on the huts' walls as flickers of flame rose and died in the fire's embers.

The old man emerged from the blackness behind the huts and walked quietly into the clearing, into the circle of waiting men. His earth-red blanket rippled as he moved and it seemed to capture yet more redness from the fire.

He stepped, with careful deliberation, over to the great, elaborately carved drum and took up position behind it.

The circle of warriors watched him, alert and expectant; a hundred eyes fixed on his tall, red-sheened figure.

The Watcher stood still for a long moment, head raised, eyes staring up into the night sky, into the heights of the mountain. Then he raised his arm high above his head. In his hand the ivory beater seemed disembodied as the black of his arm merged with the night sky. It seemed to float in air, a ghost-bone suspended by night.

The warriors waited, breath held, a circle of ebony statues frozen by expectancy.

The arm began to descend, slowly and jerkily at first. Then, with a swift arc, the beater flashed down through the black air to crash on to the membrane of the drum.

The drum gave out a deep, rolling boom. Unearthly, elemental, it hammered out from the bowl of the Ntenga and rolled in heavy, earth-vibrating waves of sound, thudding through the bodies of the watching men.

As it went it carried with it the words of the old man. Rolling on the backs of the waves of sound was his whispered, resonant voice.

'Hear the Story,' he whispered.

'Hear the Story,' repeated the warriors, in unison.

The arm raised and crashed down again. Again the booming voice of the drum and the old man's softly exhaled words mingled and shuddered outwards.

'Hear the Story of the Song.'

'Hear the Story of the Song,' the warriors replied.

A third, numbing crash of ivory on skin, and this time a shouted command from the Watcher.

'Hear the Watcher. Hear the Leopard Song.'

And the warriors repeated the command with a harsh cry, bellowed into the night.

'Hear the Watcher,' they cried. 'Hear the Leopard Song.'

The cry rose up through the night air, whirling through the forest trees on the mountain slopes.

Then the warriors fell silent as the old man turned to the two smaller drums. He seated himself on a low wooden stool between them and began to tap them with the flat of his hand.

They were different pitches, one high, the second lower and more resonant. He tapped each in turn, then paused.

Bim borrrm. Pause. Bim borrrm. Pause. Bim borrrm. A slow, rhythmic heartbeat pulsing into the night, a steady, insistent background to his voice.

'Hear the Watcher. Hear the Story.'

'In the time before this one, the time of the magic, there was in the world only the spirit, who was built of air.

'At first he was happy in the world. He would soar through the high clouds pushing them around the sky, would whistle through the rocks, and shake the trees making them dance to his breath.

'But in time he grew bored. The world was empty and only he moved in it.

'So he began to create life, from the earth itself, for his amusement. He breathed on to the waters and gave them life; the slipping currents turned into lakes of fishes. He blew warm air on to the muddy shores and moulded the baking earth into the crusted scales of crocodiles. He took the rocks of his mountain and from them shaped the rolling elephant; the river-rounded boulders he formed into the leaden hippopotami and the carved stone flags of the kopjes became the lumbering rhinoceros.

'But he was not happy. His efforts were ugly, clumsy and full of weight.

'He tried again. His breath drew up the swirling dust of the plains and settled it as the rustling lion. He blew across the swaying grasses and from them jumped the dancing gazelles and antelopes. He crashed the dark clouds of the sky together, broke them into pieces and dropped from them the birds.

'But still he was not satisfied.

'He breathed now on to the tall, straight trunks of the trees; from them stepped creatures with skin the colour of bark.

'So Man came to be. So the tribes were born, as hard and dark as trees. Each tree gave its own. From the giant fig, with its hanging roots, came the slender, lithe Maasai, whose legs can run for ever. From the yellow acacia, the fever-tree, came the ill-natured Mgubwe, the witch-people of Manyara who ride, shrieking, on hyenas in the night. From the shining jacarandas came the stately Bantu, who can steal your life-soul with their eyes. Tribe upon tribe stepped from the trees until all the world, from the White-mountain to the sea, was peopled.

'But still the Spirit was not happy. Not one of his creations satisfied him. No one was perfect.

'Now there was only one thing left from which no life had come, the great dark tree on the plains at the foot of his mountain. From this he would draw the perfect form.

'What should it be?

'It should be like himself, built of air, but given substance. It should move at the speed of wind, but with a wind's silence. It should flow like water, but be as unyielding as rock. It should be feared by all other things, but dependent on none. And its beauty should be the beauty of the world, the gold of sunlight, the black of earth.

'He breathed on to the tree, and from its branches came flowers. Tiny gold tips appeared from buds and grew and grew until the tree burst into a cloud of gold and black blossoms. The Spirit's breath touched them, floated them loose from the tree and they fell to the earth.

'The perfect form was made – the leopard – from the flowers of the Tree.

'Now the Spirit was happy. He could rest. But before he withdrew into his ice-cave he created life one final time. From the black trunk of the Tree he made one more tribe. We, the Chagga, the chosen people. Born from the same tree as the leopard; joined in birth, joined in life.

'And this the Spirit told us:

' "Now I have made my perfect form. The leopard is my spirit, the spirit of air on earth. You, the Chagga are its guardians. In time the leopard will die and others will be born from the Tree. My spirit will return with each rebirth. Each generation one of you will be born with a mark, a mark carried by no other man. He will be the guardian of the Tree. When the time of birth comes I will sing from the mountain. Those with the mark will hear my song and will do as I bid. Remember, you are the guardians. When a leopard is born, a Chagga is born. When a leopard dies, a Chagga dies. Guard the Tree well. If the Tree should die, you, the Chosen People, will die." '

The old man ceased his slow, heartbeat drumming.

He stood and faced the circle of warriors.

'The Story is told,' he said. 'The time is here. The Leopard is singing from the mountain. I have heard it. Kimathi hears it now. It is the time of rebirth. Soon the Leopard will come.'

He turned his back on them and returned to stand by the Ntenga drum.

'Go back to your huts now and wait for the Leopard.'

The men rose silently and began to make their way into the shadows. One man detached himself from the others and went and stood beside the Watcher. The old man handed him the ceremonial beater, fashioned centuries ago from the thigh-bone of a leopard; the first leopard, so the stories told. The end was covered with soft fur, colourless now with age. The warrior began to tap the drum softly.

WaChui stood and listened to the soft sound. This slow, whispered rhythm would continue now, like the breath of quiet lungs, until the Song was over and the new Watcher came to stand in his place. Soon Kimathi would come, drawn by the Song.

And together they would make the sacrifice to the Leopard.

The old man turned and walked out of the clearing and down the path towards his cave. He hoped Kimathi would come soon. He was tired now and longed to be released from his burden. He hoped Kimathi would prove himself quickly on the mountain and prayed that he would have the strength for the final sacrifice.

Kimathi did not know yet what the sacrifice had to be.

But the old man did.

And he shuddered a little with doubt as he stumbled his way down the darkened path.

twelve

It was the vibration of the earth more than the sound which woke Kimathi.

His eyes flicked open instantly, but he lay very still, almost without breathing, his mind spinning in anxious circles as he tried to work out what was happening.

A second, great crash rolled up the slopes, dull at first as though it emanated from deep in the ground, but growing in a crescendo as it hammered into the clearing. It rattled in shock waves around and around, bouncing from tree to tree.

Kimathi's stomach lurched in brief panic as the waves of sound rippled through his body.

Then, just as rapidly as they had come, they were past and muttering away off through the forest like a fading thunderclap.

Kimathi rose softly to his feet and glanced fearfully around the clearing. It was very dark, the heavy, misty darkness of deep forest. He could barely discern the trees and hanging mosses at the edges of the clearing. Everything had gone silent. A total, preternatural silence. Even the frogs had ceased their eternal grumblings and were as silent and immobile as the dead, dank leaves they squatted among.

Kimathi's hand went instinctively for his spear. With one fluid movement he bent, swept it up from the ground and straightened into a finely balanced throwing position. As the point rose up past his eyes it seemed that, for the tiniest fraction of a second, it flashed gold, as though it had caught a light and winked it back to its source. He swung his head around to the left, away from the spear, but the darkness there was as impenetrable as everywhere else. The light had not come from there.

His head whipped back again as the third wave of sound began to rumble up the slopes. But by now his sleep-numbed mind had caught up with his body. He knew what it was.

It was the drum. The great, ceremonial Ntenga was crying out from the village, hurling its voice upwards to the mountain.

Once again the sound rose through the clearing.

As it passed and began to die away through the trees Kimathi heard the words of the Watcher.

'Hear the Watcher. Hear the Leopard Song.'

He stood transfixed, trembling slightly, his eyes trying to cut into the darkness. He lowered his spear and listened. The forest was silent again, so silent he could hear his own heartbeat.

Bim borrrm. Bim borrrm. Bim borrrm.

Something was happening to him, but he couldn't say yet what it was. The spear slipped from his fingers and thudded softly on to the grass at his side.

Gradually the forest noises began to return. A solitary frog croaked a complaining lament, and behind it a stream resumed its gentle gurgle; birds shifted position in the tree-tops, rustling like paper, and fruit-bats slapped the night air with leathery wings.

Kimathi began to feel weak, as though his body was melting. He slipped down onto his hands and knees.

His heart thumped heavily in his ears.

Bim borrrm. Bim borrrm. Bim borrrm.

He lifted his head backwards and sniffed the air. He could smell the wetness of the place; the dank, heavy decay of rotting leaves and wet earth, and the wholesome fragrance of running water.

And more. As he flexed his nostrils he found messages rushed to him, each one separate so that he could easily follow it back to its source. He could smell the warm ferment of the fruit-bats folded like umbrellas high in the tree-tops. Far, far away, much higher up in the forest, he caught the sharp reek of elephant hide and the heavy, green fetor of their breath as they slept, quietly digesting a mountain of leaves. From down the slopes, far below him, the sweet rancidity of goat came up to his nose and his mouth began to salivate. He licked his lips and grunted softly.

He scanned the perimeter of the clearing. It was getting lighter and a faint, yellowish glow was beginning to bathe the nearest tree-trunks so that the blackness of those behind seemed deeper yet.

He opened his eyes wider and blinked several times. Gradually things became clearer. The yellow light grew until he could see every detail of the clearing with startling clarity. He glimpsed a tiny movement, a brief flash of colour as a snake slid, slick as oil, into a hole at the base of a trunk. He heard its dry skin rasp against the bark of a surface root and he snarled quietly, his lips drawing back over his yellow fangs.

The smell of goat was stronger now. It seeped heavily into his nostrils and lodged in the back of his throat. He swung round to pin-point its direction, the powerful sinews of his neck rippling beneath his fur, his gold eyes boring like torch beams into the forest.

And he began to move; a silent, flowing movement, undulating over the ground, dropping gradually down the mountain slopes.

Soundless though his progress was it did not go unnoticed. Here and there a monkey coughed a soft warning as the gold figure slid beneath, or sleeping eyes flicked open as his passing was felt on the air.

Within minutes he was down at the farm.

As he approached the buildings he became more cautious, creeping belly close to the ground, senses vigilant for man.

Then he stopped and crouched between the sheds. He could smell the goat strongly now but he waited, nostrils, eyes and ears seeking danger, before he made his move.

The windows of the farmhouse were dark, its occupants sleeping, but two floodlights at the front of the house lit the gardens brilliantly. He retreated behind the sheds, away from the light, and began to skirt the garden, hugging the shadows at its edges. He moved round to the back of the house where it was dark.

The goat shed sat at the edge of the garden, backing on to the rain-forest trees, and he padded up to it. He was salivating heavily now, the sharp stench of the goat blanketing the air around him, maddening him with hunger. His tongue flicked over his lips. He could almost taste the warm blood.

He heard the animal move anxiously inside the shed as it sensed his presence and he backed off silently lest it should cry out.

He eased his way into the forest behind the shed and, with an easy grace, leapt upwards into a tree. Then, with delicate steps he crept out along a branch until the soft thatch of the shed roof lay below him.

He paused a second.

The goat knew he was there and was listening too. The animal's fear rose, tangible as smoke, through the thatch. It began to move, on timid feet, around the hut, its hooves thudding dully on the earth floor.

He tried to judge its exact position within the shed, listening carefully to the sounds of its feet. His eyes scanned the thatch, following the animal's movements.

The goat stopped moving.

Now. Now he must do it.

Fixing his eyes carefully on where he must land, he braced his body. Muscles tautened like hawsers along his back. Head thrust forward he crouched slightly, legs bent, preparing for the leap.

He paused again, judging the distance.

Then the coiled-steel springs of his legs snapped open and he launched himself, rigid and arrow-straight, into the night air. He crashed through the thatch and landed directly on the goat's back.

The animal's tiny gasp of fear had no time to rise beyond its throat before it was choked off. He sunk his fangs deep into the goat's neck, encircling it and crushing it. Then, as they fell to the ground together, he gave a quick, vicious twist of his head. The goat's neck snapped with the crack of a breaking twig, a dry, deeply satisfying sound, and he felt the animal's blood seeping into his mouth slaking his terrible thirst. He held on as the goat's body and legs jerked in the rhythmic convulsions of death. Then, when it was still, he let go and stood back from it, licking his tongue across his teeth, savouring the taste of blood, exulting in the joy of the kill. His whole body vibrated with triumph.

He padded softly around the carcass, smelling the warmth of it, getting ready to lie down and feed.

Then he froze, rigid, in mid-step. His head whipped round as his acute ears picked up a noise from the direction of the house. A tiny, almost imperceptible click.

He waited.

Then came another sound, a sound which brought a growl of rage to his throat. Man sound; voices, raised and urgent, then heavy footsteps on wooden floors.

Snarling, he turned away from the noise and, with a flowing leap, catapulted himself upwards into the shed rafters. He emerged through the hole in the thatch and out on to the point of the roof.

Lights had come on inside the house and he could see figures moving about inside. His lips curled back in a hiss of disappointment and he turned to jump down on to the ground.

At that second the floodlights at the back of the house were snapped on, blinding him in their fierce light. For a moment he was startled and confused. He hesitated, not knowing which way to jump.

A tiny hesitation only, but enough for John Edwards to round the corner of the house, take a quick sight on the solitary leopard silhouetted clearly in gold against the blackness of the forest, and send a bullet hammering into it.

thirteen

The police Landcruisers drew up just after seven o'clock the next morning, their big tyres crunching on the murram of the driveway. A few seconds later Commander Makayowe's heavy boots thudded up the wooden steps and on to the veranda.

John Edwards, red-eyed from lack of sleep, was seated in an armchair waiting for him, rifle still in his hands. His wife, woken by the sound of the Landcruisers, emerged through the french windows just as Makayowe arrived. The relief was obvious on her face as she saw who it was.

'Thank God, Sebastian,' she exclaimed. 'Thank God you're here.'

'What's the matter?' Makayowe asked. 'Has something happened? Why the gun, bwana? . . .'

'We had a leopard here last night,' John Edwards replied. 'I got a shot at it, but I only wounded it and it got away. It's gone back up into the forest.'

'So,' asked Makayowe, puzzled, 'what are you worrying about? It won't come back if it's wounded. It will just creep off somewhere and either heal itself or die. No problem.'

He shrugged his shoulders dismissively.

John Edwards felt in the breast-pocket of his shirt,

pulled out a piece of paper and handed it to the commander.

'There,' he said, 'that's the problem. That was here when we got back from Moshi yesterday.'

Makayowe read the note.

'Dear Mum and Dad,

I'm going up on to the mountain. Njombo says Kimathi's there. I know all the places he's likely to go, so I'm going after him. He knows what's happening here. He'll tell me what it is, I know he will. I'll only be gone a couple of days probably. Don't worry. See you soon.

Love,
Alan.'

'It's not just the leopard we're worrying about,' Mary Edwards added. 'Things are going from bad to worse here. There was some sort of ceremony down in the village last night. They were beating a drum all night. And this morning no one's turned up for work, not even Njombo.'

'Ach,' grunted Makayowe. 'A feast. They've all drunk too much pombe and banana-beer. They're sleeping it off, that's all.'

'No, Sebastian, not a feast.' John Edwards was emphatic. 'There was no noise. No singing. They were completely quiet. Just the drum, no other noise. It was eerie. We're very worried, Sebastian, I don't mind telling you. And now, to cap it all, our son's up there on that blasted mountain with a wounded leopard roaming about. I'll tell you that frightens us to death.'

'It's a big mountain, bwana, they won't meet up.'

'I know. We keep telling ourselves that. But we're not convincing ourselves.' He reached out and took his wife's hand. 'I've been sitting here all night feeling completely helpless. It's no good me following Alan. I've no idea where he and Kimathi go up there. They never take the climbers' tracks. They have their own routes, their own places. I wouldn't know where to start. And anyway I can't leave the farm. Goodness only knows what these village people have in mind, but whatever it is, it's dangerous.'

He gazed anxiously out over the garden and on to the mountain slopes. His tiredness had made him look defeated, smaller somehow than the John Edwards Makayowe knew so well.

And Makayowe too was finding himself to be a little anxious. His loyalties were pulling. These people were his friends, people he had liked and respected for twenty years. He wanted to protect them. It was his duty to protect them; that was the life he had chosen and the uniform he wore was its symbol.

But the man inside the uniform was an African, and that loyalty pulled the other way. His roots were still in African soil and, though he could convince himself that he was an educated man, above the superstitious beliefs of the village tribespeople, what would he do when his two loyalties pulled with equal strength?

The Chagga had marked this house for sacrifice,

that much he knew. But what they believed the sacrifice would achieve he did not know. The Chagga guarded their secrets carefully. What if he were to stop these events, as he knew he had the power to do? Would he then be betraying his own countrymen, betraying Africa?

He wanted to tell John Edwards to take his wife and son and leave this place. They weren't of this world anyway. They were white and need have no part in the tales told by the tribes.

But he did not have the courage yet to tell them to run away. He decided to shelve the problem until he knew more. He decided to be, for the moment anyway, just a policeman. The African receded.

'So,' he said, leaning back in his chair and thumping the arms decisively, 'things look bad. You are both tired. Go, sleep a while and things will change. While you sleep, Makayowe will work.'

He thudded on to his feet and stepped out to the edge of the veranda.

'Sergeant,' he bellowed out over the garden.

'Sir,' yelped a startled voice.

'Get those idle scoundrels who have the impertinence to call themselves policemen out of those Landcruisers and across here. Now.'

'Yes, sir.'

There was a hurried clicking of doors, urgent whisperings, and the frantic drumming of boots on turf as the men dashed across to the house. When Makayowe said 'now' he meant it, and any laggard could expect a fearful cuff to the ear if he was one second behind the others.

In an instant ten uniformed officers stood in a perfect line, rigidly to attention, rifles at their sides, wary eyes fixed on their commander, awaiting instructions.

'So,' said Makayowe, 'we have some small work to do.'

He surveyed them contemptuously, eyes moving slowly along the line.

'The work is not hard, so perhaps even you, the worst of police, who are not fit even to clean the boots of real policemen, may succeed.'

He singled out a tall, young constable.

'You, Obote. Forward.'

The man jumped one pace forward and immediately became ram-rod straight again.

'Sir?'

'You have, I believe, some small talent in tracking?'

The man nodded.

'Small though your skills undoubtedly are, you are the best we have. The boy, Alan Edwards, is on the mountain. Also on the mountain is the boy Kimathi of Marangu village. Take one man with you, find them and bring them home.'

'Yes, sir,' replied the constable.

'If,' added Makayowe, 'you do not find them, do not come back here, for you will not wish to see me again. Sergeant!'

'Sir.'

'Select the three strongest men from these weaklings and go down to the village. There you will knock some heads together and get those idle people back up here to work, where they belong. If any man resists tie him to an anthill and he will change his mind.'

'Yes, sir,' bellowed the sergeant.

'The rest of you will guard the house. Allow no man to come near the house until I return. No man at all. If any harm comes to Bwana or Mama Edwards you will pay with your skins. Now, move.'

The men moved immediately.

The commander turned again and addressed his friends.

'So,' he said, 'now things are better. Please, go to bed and rest. Leave this to me; I will solve this problem. Sleep easy, the Bantu is a fine tracker. He will find Alan quickly. Tonight he will be home.'

'I believe you, Sebastian,' said Mary Edwards with a small smile. 'Your tracker wouldn't dare come back without him.'

John rose from the chair.

'Thank you, Sebastian. I don't know what we would have done without you. I was beginning to think . . .'

His voice trailed off wearily.

'Don't think, bwana, sleep. Makayowe is in charge now.'

'Right, we will. I'm about done in. We'll talk later. Thank you again.'

He turned, put his arm around his wife's shoulders, and they walked into the house through the french windows.

Makayowe watched them go and again felt sorry for them. They looked now much older than their years. He waited for a moment until his men had taken up their positions around the house. When he was satisfied that the house was well protected, he crossed the garden and headed for the path which led down to the village. For the moment things were in order. Makayowe the policeman was doing his duty.

But the dilemma remained. How much more should he do?

The African in him began to nag again.

He needed to be able to see things more clearly. Find out exactly what the Chagga were doing, and why.

And only one man could tell him that: the old man they called WaChui.

fourteen

The bullet had passed through Kimathi's calf muscle but, fortunately, had missed the bone. The leg had hurt dreadfully but he had still been able to walk.

When he had limped back into the forest clearing he had bathed the wound in the cool waters of the stream. Then he had packed it with the healing moss which hangs from the rain-trees, bound it with strips of leaf torn from the banana plant, and slept.

When dawn broke he found that the soft moss had eased the pain to a dull throb.

He stood and tested the leg, taking a few, uncertain paces around the clearing. Then, satisfied that it would support him he prepared to leave.

His anxieties had eased too, and he felt relaxed. He gathered the leopard-skin cloak under his arm, picked up his spear and set off down the mountain. He was confident that the Watcher would be pleased with him. He had heard the Song, followed it where it had led him and done what it had demanded.

He had killed in the night, as leopards had done from time beyond memory. Now it was over and he could go back down to the village, take his place by the Tree, guard over it and wait to tell the Story to the new Watcher of the next generation.

It had not, after all, been too hard, the Song not too demanding. Perhaps now his life could get back to normal. He knew that now, like the old man, he would never be able to leave the cave. The Tree must never be left unguarded. But he would see the people of the village and his family. Perhaps, even, he would be able to see Alan again.

So, for a time, he was light-hearted and, in spite of the wound, he moved easily and confidently down the hidden path towards the village.

His mood did not last for long.

As he approached the Edwards's farm he heard the noise of engines and the crunch of tyres on murram. He skirted the farm and edged through the forest just below it so that he could see what was happening. Hidden behind a large tree he peered out from the shadows.

He saw the three Landcruisers parked at angles in front of the house and watched as a large, blue-uniformed figure ascended the steps to the veranda.

Makayowe. What was he doing here?

He saw the police commander sit and talk quietly with Alan's father. He could not hear what they were saying but he caught one or two words. He heard his own name mentioned. He strained his ears but could not pick up what they were saying about him.

His confidence began to ebb. What was happening? John Edwards would not have brought the police just because of a goat. Perhaps somebody had reported the shot and the police had called to check. But the commander wouldn't have come himself only for a gunshot, he would have sent a couple of constables.

He began to feel uneasy. Perhaps there were things he did not know. Perhaps there was something the Watcher had not told him.

He saw Makayowe rise to his feet and step forwards to the front of the veranda.

This time Kimathi heard his words as the man bellowed out his commands to his men.

'The boy, Alan Edwards, is on the mountain. Also on the mountain is the boy Kimathi . . .' he heard. 'Bring them home.'

Kimathi went cold and a surging anger rolled up through him from the pit of his stomach. This man, Makayowe, was betraying him. This man, an African, was telling his men to go up to the mountain and bring him down. What did he think he was doing? It was inconceivable that an African would interfere with tribal lore.

Kimathi's eyes darkened with rage. Makayowe would destroy everything.

His brain began to race. What could he do?

He wanted to raise his spear and hurl it into this hateful man's body. But he did nothing. Makayowe had too many men with him, and their guns frightened him. They would kill him even if Makayowe didn't.

He withdrew deeper into the trees and waited. He would tell the Watcher. He would know what to do, how to stop this meddling.

Kimathi resumed his journey down to the cave but stopped when he heard the commander order his men down to the village. He remained still and listened carefully. Shortly he heard the men's footsteps as they thudded down the path, their boots squelching in the wet earth.

He waited, uncertain now what to do, cursing Makayowe, his heart sinking as he began to wonder if perhaps he was the cause of this. Had it been his carelessness which had brought the police?

The Song had told him to kill, but perhaps he had been wrong to kill so close to people. Especially white people, who made more fuss if their stock fell victim to wild animals.

And he had been seen. Was that it? John Edwards had seen him clearly enough to shoot and wound him. Was that a failure? Had he exposed the leopard-spirit to danger, to the scrutiny of men who should not be allowed to know?

And had he been wrong this morning in thinking that it was all over, that he had done his part and the Spirit was satisfied with him?

Perhaps there was another test yet to come.

Perhaps Makayowe was the test.

He heard a set of boots approaching so he crept out to where he would be able to see the path. The sound came nearer and he pulled aside the swathes of moss to look out.

Makayowe.

Anger bubbled up again and his eyes filled with hatred as they settled on the commander.

Makayowe. Alone.

His mind whirled. What was he supposed to do? The Song had not allowed him to think for himself;

it had taken him, guided him along the path it wanted him to go. But the Song was silent now. This decision he was thinking out for himself. This was Kimathi and Makayowe, man against man.

He brought up his spear and pulled his arm back into a throwing position. He had to decide quickly or the moment would be gone, the opportunity lost. He flexed the muscles of his arm, preparing to throw. The commander drew level with him, then passed, presenting his broad back directly to Kimathi's searching eyes.

He took aim. Now. Now he must do it.

But his arm did not move. The spear remained, poised. For behind him he heard a noise. The faintest of rustlings only, but enough to give him pause. A whispering through the denseness of the forest, like a soft wind. A cold, sighing breath, carrying upon it the ice of the high peaks of Kibo, freezing him into immobility.

'No,' whispered a voice on the breath. 'Not yet.'

'No,' said the Song, 'this is not him.'

And then, as suddenly as it had come, it was gone. Warmth returned to the forest and the commander, briefly glancing around and shaking his head, carried on down the path.

As the sound of the man's feet receded Kimathi slumped down, back against a tree and leaned his head dispiritedly on to his knees.

So. It was not over.

He had been wrong.

'Not yet. This is not him,' the Song had said.

So there was another test. Another 'him'. The

night-dream baboon of Serengeti, the goat, they had been preparation only. The real test was yet to come and the Song would guide him to it.

Suddenly Kimathi felt very afraid.

fifteen

Long before Makayowe reached the village he knew something was wrong. There was no noise.

His men would be there now, rounding up the workers, pushing people into line at gunpoint, cuffing surly heads and letting fly with boots.

He paused on the path and listened. There were no yells of protest or screams of pain or shouted commands. Only the soft forest noises; moisture dripping from trees; the quiet rustlings of wary creatures; and, in the background, the quiet pulsing of a drum.

The commander's eyes flashed with anger. Was it conceivable that his men had disobeyed him? No one disobeyed Makayowe. What the devil were they doing? He would break their heads, along with the heads of half the villagers.

He continued down the path and by the time he strode into the village he was in a high rage and ready to knock his sergeant to the floor.

The scene which greeted him as he rounded a hut and stepped into the clearing drove that thought from his mind and froze him in his tracks. Everything was so still, so silent, that it surprised him and he had to pause to take it in.

A cloud had obscured the sun and washed the colour from the village. Grey smoke from the dying fire hung, like strands of hair, over the clearing and seeped outwards, creeping up the walls of the huts and fingering through the thatch.

Around the edges of the clearing, in a great circle, sat the men of the village, their oiled bodies shining like polished ebony, the gold of their body decoration the only glow of colour relieving the pervading greys and blacks. Their faces, painted into grotesque masks, were expressionless. Their eyes stared straight ahead, unseeing and lifeless.

At the far end of the circle a single warrior gave the only movement to the chilling scene as his arm rose and fell in a long, slow rhythm drawing a soft sound from the drum.

Makayowe's eyes searched the clearing for his men. They were grouped, disconsolate and fearful, in the shadows of a hut at the far side of the village. The scene had defeated them. They had no idea what to do.

Nor, for the moment, had Makayowe.

He looked again at the warriors, shook his head in doubt and stepped over to the nearest of them.

They were so still that he could hardly believe they were alive; but as he stared hard at them he saw that they were indeed breathing. The slightest of movements only, as the sigh of the drum beat wafted a breath into their bodies and the next beat took it away again.

He pushed one of the men in the back with his boot.

'You,' he said, 'get up.'

The man did not move at all; made no sign that he was even aware of Makayowe's presence.

A flash of anger crossed the commander's eyes and he aimed a heavy kick between the man's shoulder-blades. The warrior lurched forward with the impact, but made no sound. He slowly raised himself up again until he was sitting exactly as before. Not the slightest flicker of expression crossed his face.

Makayowe was incensed.

'I told you to get up, you snivelling snake,' he screamed and, reaching down, he grabbed hold of the man's tightly curled hair and hauled him viciously to his feet. Holding him at arm's length he bellowed into his face.

'I gave you an order you miserable dung-beetle. When I speak you will . . .'

His voice trailed off. The man was not looking at him, not hearing him. His eyes remained completely without expression; fixed, vacant and far, far away. The man inside the body was not there.

Makayowe released him. He simply slumped down again, resuming his position as before.

The commander stepped back, uncertain. He was beginning, like his men, to feel out of his depth.

Crime he could handle. Vicious murderers he regarded as no threat at all. He had quelled riots single-handed and bludgeoned rebellious tribesmen into submission armed only with fists and feet.

But this. This was different. And, in spite of himself, he felt a chill rising up his backbone. These men were entranced, held in a spell. Their eyes were fixed on something he could not see. They were oblivious to him.

How do you deal with people who can't see you; who don't know you're there?

This was magic. The thought passed through Makayowe's mind that no man, not even he, could fight magic.

Instantly he was contemptuous of himself for even thinking it, for allowing doubt to creep into his mind.

Of course he could deal with this. The magic was only in the minds of these ignorant tribespeople. He had long ago grown away from such beliefs and they had no part in his life now. He was an educated, twentieth-century man, and the twentieth century had no place for magic. Magic was for savages, and Makayowe was not going to be defeated by savages.

'So,' he whispered to himself, 'it will be ended. The cycle will be broken. And I, Makayowe, will break it.'

He signalled across the clearing to his men. They came running anxiously around the edge of the clearing and up to him. Their eyes betrayed the fact that they were on unsure ground. They needed their commander's confidence.

As usual they got his contempt.

'You trembling girls,' he spat at them, 'cowering in the shadows like beaten dogs waiting for their master to pat them. Why have you not moved these men as I told you?'

'Sir,' said the sergeant, quivering slightly, 'they will not move. We kick them and they show no pain.

We lift them and they fall again. These men, sir, are not alive.'

'Of course they are alive you snivelling toad. Look, they breathe.'

Makayowe grabbed the sergeant by the scruff of his neck and pushed his head down close to one of the seated warriors.

'See. They breathe, so they are alive.'

'Yes, sir.'

The sergeant rubbed his bruised neck ruefully as Makayowe released him.

'And if you wish to remain alive,' hissed the commander, 'if you wish to breathe, you will obey my orders. These men are drugged. They are in a trance, and the one with the drum controls them. You, Sergeant will arrest him. Take him back up to the farm and handcuff him to the Landcruiser.'

The sergeant saluted.

'Yes, sir,' he replied, briskly.

He turned and walked, rifle at the ready, towards the man beating the Ntenga.

'The rest of you wait here. When the men come out of their trance march them back up to the coffee slopes and get them back to work. I will go down the hill and speak with the old man, WaChui.'

'Yes, sir,' chorused the constables.

They moved off and positioned themselves around the clearing.

Makayowe crossed the clearing too and set off down the path towards the old man's cave.

He strode confidently now, for the small doubts he had had about where his loyalties lay were settled.

They lay not with his friend, John Edwards, though he would benefit from Makayowe's decision. Nor did they lie with Makayowe the policeman, though the law would certainly be upheld. Not even with his tribal, African blood, for he was, he now knew, no longer part of the old ways.

No.

His real loyalty, he had found, was to himself and to his own pride. No one had ever beaten Sebastian Makayowe, and no one was going to beat him now.

No one and no thing.

Not even magic.

'And that,' said Makayowe to himself, 'is that.'

Behind him, in the ghost-grey clearing, the sergeant reached out, grasped the arm which held the leopard-skinned drumstick, and stopped the drum. The Chagga warrior's face did not change at all at the interruption and, like all the others, he gave no sign that he knew the policeman was there.

From high on the mountain there was a soft rumble of building thunder as the morning clouds gathered around Kibo.

The drum missed one beat only. With a casual flick of the arm, almost as though he were unconsciously brushing away a fly, the warrior threw off the sergeant's grip and resumed beating.

Angrily the sergeant grasped his arm again, more firmly.

'You,' he shouted. 'You are under arrest.'

The warrior's arm tried to descend to keep the rhythm of the drumbeat. When he encountered resistance, again without any change of expression, he flicked his arm back, this time with much greater force. The sergeant was thrown off balance and staggered backwards.

Another beat was missed.

The low thunder grumbled again from the mountain, but deeper, more menacing.

And slowly, so slowly that it was imperceptible to the three policemen standing at the edges of the clearing, the still statues of the other warriors began to turn their heads, eyes blank but searching.

The drum resumed, the warrior beating it unperturbed and unaware.

The sergeant was furious now.

Swinging his rifle up he gave the man a ferocious crack to the back of the head with the butt.

'Listen to me when I speak,' he screamed.

The warrior staggered, slumped to his knees and fell forward on to his face.

A great crack of thunder shuddered across the sky.

Startled by the sound the sergeant turned away from the fallen body and looked around. What he saw stopped his heart and a harsh scream of terror bubbled up to his throat.

The warriors had risen to their feet and were advancing on his men. Still without expression of any sort they moved slowly, stiffly, like machines, their blank eyes fixed with implacable purpose on their quarries. In their hands glinted wicked, curved knives.

His men seemed transfixed, unable to move, like birds mesmerized by the eyes of a snake. Their faces were contorted in terror but they did not raise their guns or make any effort to run.

There were not even any screams as the knives flashed repeatedly in the air and the warriors, with silent, automaton efficiency, killed the policemen.

Frozen to the ground with horror, the sergeant tried to raised his gun but found that he could not.

Beside him the warrior he had clubbed to the ground had risen to his feet again, raised his arm, and begun to beat the drum as though nothing had happened.

The rumbling thunder receded into the distance.

The sergeant watched, in helpless silence, as the warriors, with the slowness of a dream and the numbing horror of a nightmare, walked towards him.

When the killing was over the men returned to their huts to collect their spears. Then, in a strange, ghostly line, they left the village and began to make their way up the mountain.

When they were gone the women crept out from the huts, dragged the bodies of the policemen into the forest, and hid them.

The thunder on the mountain stilled.

sixteen

The meeting between WaChui and Makayowe was short and explosive.

'Whatever you're telling your people to do,' Makayowe had said, 'stop it now, or I will stop it for you.'

WaChui was astonished that an African could speak that way.

'I tell them nothing, you know that. What they do is what the tribe has always done. The Spirit tells them what they must do, not I.'

'Your tribe can believe what it wants to believe,' Makayowe replied. 'And if you had kept this thing amongst yourselves then I would not be here. This is different. You have involved others.'

'We have no choice. The Spirit gives us no choice.'

'And now I give you no choice,' Makayowe snapped. 'These people are white people. They have nothing to do with you. They are not of Africa. Leave them alone.'

'But you,' said WaChui, 'you are of Africa. You know you cannot alter the ways of the tribes.'

The commander scoffed.

'You are old and live in a different time. There are new ways now.'

WaChui shook his head.

'Not for us. Not for the Chagga. We have to follow the path we are given.'

Makayowe began to lose patience. He pushed his face up to WaChui's and snarled at him.

'Hear me, old man. So far you have only frightened the white family. Stop things now and no harm will be done. Continue and I will lock up every man of your tribe until they change their minds. Already I am clearing the village and sending your people back to work. The farm is guarded. Should any man go near it he will be shot.'

WaChui was calmly defiant.

'You must do what you must do, bwana,' he replied. 'But so must we. I have no power to stop you. But neither have I the power to stop the tribe.'

'They will listen to you. Tell them,' insisted Makayowe.

'No, Commander, they will not listen to me. My time is over.'

'Who then? Who do they listen to now?'

'Ah, that, bwana, you must find out for yourself.'

He turned as though to go inside his cave, but Makayowe grabbed him by the shoulder and stopped him.

'It's the boy, isn't it? Kimathi. Bwana Edwards says he is up on the mountain. What does he do there?'

WaChui brushed off the commander's hand and stared hard at him.

'Makayowe,' he said, 'go back to Moshi. Let things take their course. Kimathi only does what he is being told to do. Why do you interfere? This is tribal, stay out of it.'

'No, mzee, I cannot. When you marked the Edwards's farm you brought me into it. Kill each other if you wish, that's tribal, and that has nothing to do with me. But no one touches the white man or his family. No one, or you will answer to me. Do you understand me, old man?'

WaChui shrugged but did not reply.

The two men glared at each other briefly, then WaChui turned away and began to walk back towards his cave.

Makayowe watched him go and shook his head in disbelief. How could stubborn old fools like this still exist? Still cling to tales of spirits and magic? How, in this time, in this century, could anyone be so simple as to believe such things?

He turned and set off back up the path to the village.

It didn't matter anyway. He would put an end to this nonsense once and for all.

When he passed through the village again he smiled with satisfaction. Apart from a few skeletal chickens mindlessly tapping the earth with their beaks, and some bony, dejected-looking curs licking the abandoned cooking pots, it was deserted. As it should be at this time of day.

His men had obviously driven the villagers up on to the coffee slopes and got them back to work. Good. That was one thing dealt with.

Soon the Bantu trackers would bring Alan and Kimathi down, then he could lock Kimathi up, along with anyone else who wanted to give trouble, and that would be an end of this thing. In time the villagers would see the error of their ways and it would all be forgotten.

All he had to do now was wait, and he could do that sitting comfortably on the farm veranda while his friend slept some of his worries away.

But his satisfaction was short-lived, for as he came up the last rise before the farm and looked across to the coffee slopes he could see that they, like the village, were deserted.

He stopped and listened carefully. There was no sound at all, no movement of any sort.

He quickened his pace, shocked that his orders had once more been disobeyed, almost disbelieving this failure.

He hurried now, alarmed at the turn of events and by the time he reached the house he was almost running. Immediately he came through the farm gateway he flicked a glance at the buildings and around the gardens. They too were deserted and silent. The four men he had left on guard were gone.

He came to a halt abruptly, fighting down his flaring rage. He narrowed his eyes, looking for danger, scanning around the perimeters of the garden. Then, drawing his revolver, he started to walk slowly towards the house. His eyes moved from side to side as he went, searching the forest at the garden's edge.

He passed the abandoned Landcruisers parked on the grass at the front of the house and paused a second at the foot of the veranda steps, listening for noises. The house too was silent.

He was just about to ascend the steps and call out to John Edwards when a tiny movement, seen only in the corner of his eye, stopped him. A brief shifting of shadows in the trees, away to his right across the garden.

Someone was watching him.

He stopped the instinctive swing of his head just in time. He must not let the hidden watcher know that he was aware of his presence or the figure would melt and vanish into the forest before he had time to reach him. Instead he turned his head the other way and began to walk slowly around to the side of the house, away from the hiding figure.

As soon as he rounded the corner and was out of sight he began to move quickly. He rapidly unlaced his heavy boots, tore off his socks and padded, barefoot and silent, into the forest. Then, as delicate and quiet as a cat, he began to circle round, slipping from shadow to shadow, tree to tree, to get behind the lurking watcher

He found him quickly. The man was still standing where Makayowe had seen him, well back from the garden, peering out carefully and attentively. He was waiting for the commander to emerge around the side of the house again, quite unaware that he had been tricked and that the watcher was now watched.

Makayowe inched forward silently until he was directly behind the man, a few feet only separating them.

He raised his revolver and pointed it at the back of the man's head.

'Remain exactly where you are, snake,' he hissed.

The man lurched forward, startled, but froze again instantly.

'Take one step and I will kill you.'

The man began to tremble slightly but did as he was ordered. He made no move at all.

Still keeping the gun trained on the man's head, Makayowe moved towards him. When he was within arm's length he reached out, grabbed the man's collar and pushed him violently out through the trees and into the garden.

The man cried out in fear.

'Please, bwana, do not kill me. I do no harm. Please.'

Makayowe flung him headlong on to the grass. He lay face down, quivering with fear.

'No, bwana, please. Please do not kill me.'

The commander stood over the man's outstretched body, legs apart, revolver held steady in both hands, taking stock.

'Silence,' he bellowed, 'or I will kill you now, you miserable snake.'

The figure on the ground stopped its terrified pleading but continued to moan quietly with fear.

Makayowe stared hard at him. He hadn't been able to see him clearly in the dimness of the forest. Now, out in the sunlight, his captive was revealed to be a small, grey-haired, old man.

Makayowe snorted and relaxed. The figure posed no threat at all. Just a puny old man.

He returned the gun to its holster then leaned down, hauled the man up on to his feet by his shirt and turned him round.

The old man raised his arms to protect his head, fearful of the commander's great, bunched fist.

'Now,' snarled Makayowe, 'we will see what we can learn from you.'

'Please, I have done nothing wrong. Please, let me go.'

'If you have done nothing wrong,' the commander hissed from between clenched teeth, 'then you have nothing to fear. But,' his tone became even more menacing, 'if you have done nothing wrong why do you slither in the trees like the snakes? Who are you? What are you doing here?'

'Please,' the man's voice was weak with fear, 'please, I am Njombo, servant to Bwana Edwards.'

Makayowe looked hard at him, sensing that he was telling the truth but not relaxing his vice-like grip on the man's shirt.

'Perhaps,' he snarled. 'So, why does the servant of Bwana Edwards hide when he sees a policeman? You were watching me. Hiding from me. Why?'

He swung Njombo round and started to march him towards the house.

'Come,' he said, 'we will talk to Bwana Edwards. We will see what you have done that you should hide.'

John Edwards had already emerged sleepily on to the veranda, woken by the yelps of fear and Makayowe's bellowing voice.

'What is it,' he asked. 'What's happening now?'

'Many things are happening, Bwana John. Serious things. The villagers have all gone, I do not know where. My men are gone too. And this man hides in the bush near your house. Do you know him?'

'Of course,' John Edwards replied with surprise. 'Njombo, what are you doing?'

The old man stood trembling fearfully, eyes cast down on to the ground, unable to look John Edwards in the face. He remained silent.

Makayowe nudged him heavily with his elbow and Njombo yelped.

'Come on,' said John Edwards, gently, 'there's no need to be afraid of me, Njombo. You know that. Why were you hiding?'

'Oh, bwana,' he replied, almost tearful now, 'I do not hide from you, or from the police. I hide from the village. I hide because I am afraid of what is happening. Of what will happen.'

'So.' said the commander. 'Now we come to it.'

'I have been hiding since yesterday. Since I warned Bwana Alan that you must all go away. I feared that the men would find out that I had spoken and would kill me for it.'

His voice broke with emotion and he began to sob.

'And now Bwana Alan is on the mountain, and I am more afraid.'

John Edwards's face became set and he turned pale. He reached out and gripped the man's arm very tightly, suddenly desperately afraid. What was this man saying?

'What, Njombo? What is it? What are you telling me?'

'Oh, bwana, I can hide no longer. I can be silent no longer. My heart breaks for you.'

'Njombo,' shouted John Edwards, 'for heaven's sake what are you saying?'

Njombo opened his mouth to speak again, but Makayowe intervened.

'It's all right old man,' he said quietly, 'that's enough. I understand what you say.'

'I'm damned if I do,' snapped John Edwards, angrily. He shook Njombo. 'Speak up, damn you. Tell me what you know. Tell me what it is.'

'Leave him, Bwana John', Makayowe said. 'Leave him be. If he speaks they will kill him. He knows it and I know it. And it will serve no purpose. I can tell you what you wish to know. Go back to the village old man. Do not fear any more. I will stop this thing.'

A faint flicker of hope rose to Njombo's eyes.

'Can you?' he asked.

'I will stop it.'

The old man looked again at John Edwards, his eyes anguished and tear-filled.

'Forgive us, Bwana John', he whispered. 'Forgive us.'

Then he turned and left, hurrying away through the garden, his shoulders hunched with his unhappiness and shame.

John Edwards looked enquiringly and anxiously at the commander.

'What?' he asked. 'What will you stop?'

Inside himself he thought he knew the answer, but a deep dread kept the thought down.

'Come inside,' replied Makayowe, 'and I will tell you what I believe is happening. Then together we must go and bring Alan home.'

seventeen

WaChui sighed heavily as he descended the path into the lower cave.

Makayowe had distressed him. To question the power of the Spirit was beyond understanding, yet here was this man, not only questioning but declaring that he would intervene.

The arrogance of the man was boundless. What did he believe? That his ridiculous twentieth-century uniform carried a power greater than that of the Chagga tribe? His uniform signalled enslavement, nothing more. It was given by the white man. And now Makayowe was turning his back on tribal law and upholding white man's law. He was no longer an African. He was a white man in a black skin.

He must not be allowed to interfere.

The sacrifice must take place as it always had. The Leopard demanded it. That was written.

The sacrifice must always be from outside the tribe, not one of the Chosen People, and must be one born on the same day as the One with the Mark. That was inescapable.

And now they were nearly at that day.

Kimathi's mark was there for all to see. But the other boy, Alan Edwards, carried a mark too, as indelible, as unequivocal as Kimathi's. Not visible, but there nevertheless, deep inside him.

Alan could not hear the Song, but it was guiding him up the mountain as surely as it guided Kimathi.

Ever present, it had drawn both their lives to this moment.

This now was the test of the tribe's strength, of their fitness to be guardians of the Leopard Spirit. The One with the Mark had never failed. He must not fail now.

Makayowe must be stopped. But how? He was a very powerful figure, and behind him were ranged rank upon rank of men who would have no sympathy with the fate of the Chagga tribe. They would obey Makayowe's orders unquestioningly, mindlessly wielding their guns.

The old man shook his head sadly as he arrived in the dim cavern deep below the ground. He could feel defeat in the air and was disturbed and frightened by it. His life should now be coming to a calm, predetermined conclusion as his long vigil moved to its close. This should be a time of rejoicing, of grateful relief, as the weight of his lifelong burden transferred to other, younger shoulders.

But now there was too much uncertainty, too much doubt, and perhaps the fault was his.

He tried to think back. *Was* the mistake his? Should he have been able to foresee these dangers? And if he had foreseen them, would he have been able to do anything about them?

Things had been harder for him than any of the watchers before him. The coming of the white man had made them harder. In one lifetime they had brought more change than a thousand years of history. WaChui cursed his luck that they had come in his time, casting their seeds of doubt upon Africa, tempting people away from their beliefs.

He shuffled across the dusty floor and sat down on a rock close to the ebony warrior. He needed reassurance, and here in this secret, hidden place was all the history of the tribe, the words of the Story embedded deeply into the very rocks surrounding him, infused into the stone by a thousand, thousand whispered tellings.

The warrior was just visible, a single ray of cold morning light faintly illuminating the wall behind him so that he stood in soft-edged, sepia silhouette. Shorn of his leopard skins he looked smaller, less impressive, his spearless, raised arm a futile, meaningless gesture.

The old man sighed again as he looked at him. This warrior too, like the cave itself, carried in him the history of the tribe, the hard wood threaded through with taut sinews of Chagga pride.

Was it only imagination which made him look diminished? Was the old man's doubt making the figure less sure, less resolute, his stance shorn of authority?

The light increased slightly as the sun shifted position. The wall behind the warrior lightened and the soft edges of his silhouette became more distinct, hardening into clearer, sharper lines.

WaChui's eyes scanned the figure, hoping he would find a message of reassurance boring through the cave roof, would draw a message down from the Spirit. Draw it down and spill it into the darkness surrounding them and show him the way to be rid of doubt.

But the figure gave nothing back to him. It remained a silent silhouette, lifeless as the wood from which it was made, empty of threat, and of message.

WaChui let his eyes gradually descend from the figure's head, examining the outline of the torso, then onwards down the legs.

The old man started slightly.

Something was wrong. The stance was not quite the same, had lost its sure familiarity. Something about the warrior's legs was not right, something WaChui couldn't really see but which jarred him nevertheless.

He rose and went over to the figure. He examined the right leg carefully, running his hands over the metal-smooth wood. Nothing.

His hands moved to the other leg and, as they rose up from the ankle and over the calf muscle, they began to tremble.

The statue was damaged. WaChui's searching fingers found themselves delicately probing splintered wood.

He gasped in shock as he stared hard at the leg. He could see light seeping through a small hole. Something had pierced right through it.

He scrambled to his feet, brain whirling as he tried to make sense of this terrible thing. How could this have happened? No one knew of this place except Kimathi and him. No one could have been here; yet the statue, the very life-symbol of the Chagga, was damaged, desecrated. What could it mean?

He slumped down on to a stone, his head in his hands. Terribly dismayed he concentrated on the appalling event, his old mind racing back through the years to when he was young and first learning the Story. Had he forgotten something? Was there something he should have done, but had failed to do; and this was the result?

But he could think of nothing which would account for it. Damage to the statue had no part in the Story for it was unthinkable that it could ever occur.

And now it had happened, in his time, in his guardianship; and he was ashamed that it had, yet powerless to know what he could have done to prevent it, or what he should do now.

Wearily he pulled himself to his feet and turned to make his way back across the cave towards the tunnel; but before he reached the black gash of its entrance he stopped, arrested by a small sound. The soft sound of bare feet descending from the cave above. Slow, careful steps exploring the unfamiliarity of the stone floor.

He waited quietly, glad that Kimathi was returning. The Leopard Spirit was sending the boy back to him, so he had passed his first test. Now he must learn the truth of the sacrifice.

Kimathi emerged and began to walk across the cave towards him. Even in the subdued light WaChui could see that the boy was limping. The old man's eyes flicked instantly to the dragging leg, its calf muscle swollen to grotesque size by the dressing of moss and leaves.

They stood facing each other in the dead hush of the cave. The old man and the young, caught in a spell of silence, both uncertain, both afraid of what the next hours held.

The old man turned and looked again at the carved statue. The light had increased slightly.

WaChui gasped and stepped forward.

Surely he was mistaken? Surely this could not be?

He took another step forward to be sure he was not deceived.

There was no mistake. A thin, slow trickle of blood was seeping from the hole in the warrior's leg and creeping, snake-like, inexorably down towards the ankle. And on the shoulder, unnoticed earlier in the dim light, two deep fang-wounds glared redly, like mad hyena eyes, a soft flow of blood weeping from them too.

WaChui turned back to the silent, bewildered Kimathi.

'Oh, Kimathi,' he said, 'my poor Kimathi. Come. First we will ease your wounds. Then we will go, together, and do what has to be done.'

He started to lead Kimathi back towards the tunnel to the upper cave.

'Ease your mind too. It is nearly over. Tomorrow it will be finished.'

eighteen

Things didn't go exactly as Alan had planned. He'd
overslept and woken very annoyed with himself, just
before dawn. Then he had made two mistakes.

In his hurry to leave he had decided not to eat any
breakfast but had just nibbled a couple of dry biscuits
as he made his way up through the last few hundred
feet of rain forest and emerged on to the long stretch
of moorland. That was his first mistake.

His second, much more serious, was to hurry.
Anxious to keep to his self-imposed schedule he had
rushed, almost run in places, driving himself too
hard, forgetting that the mountain always exacts a
harsh revenge on the impetuous.

He had covered the moorland stretch from Mandara to Horombo in under five hours. Common sense,
if he had been listening to it, would have told him
to take seven.

'Pole, pole', the porters say. 'Take it slow.' Give
time for the body to adjust, to find its balance, in the
ever-diminishing air.

He had not heeded the first nagging signs, and the
mountain had paid him back. By the time he reached
Horombo Hut, at over thirteen thousand feet, his
body had betrayed him. He had a thumping head-

ache, felt strangely disorientated and disembodied and, periodically, heaved with nausea.

He knew what it was immediately and was angry with himself for having allowed it to happen. He should have known better. He had seen this a thousand times as over-enthusiastic, gasping climbers were stretchered down the mountain slopes by long-suffering porters; porters with knowing, unsympathetic smiles on their faces, who would shake their heads wisely and murmur, 'Haraka, bwana, haraka'.

Too much hurry.

He had altitude sickness. And that, brought about by his own thoughtless stupidity, had baulked his plan.

He knew that he must not, dare not, attempt to go any higher. There are only two cures for altitude sickness. Go down again, which was unthinkable now that he had come so far. Or wait, rest, until the symptoms pass; until the heart slows, the gasping breaths calm, and the aches and nausea recede. Wait for the body to learn to function in the debilitating thinness of the high air.

So, angry as he was with himself, he was resigned to the fact that the long trek across the saddle to Kibo Hut would have to wait until tomorrow. He would have to while away the afternoon sitting in the sun outside the huts, feeling sorry for himself and hoping that he would start to feel better soon.

If his mission had been less urgent he would have enjoyed the hours, for Horombo is a place of startling majesty.

Mawenzi, east peak of Kilima Njaro, rears behind

the huts, its saw-toothed pinnacles ripping long rents in the white clouds. Tortured by the ferocious African sun by day and ice cracked in the cold of night, Mawenzi creaks and groans as its soft rocks strain and crack and crumble. Great pieces of it let go their hold and fall, thundering down ravines and gullies, to shatter in great dust-clouds. It is a dying mountain, its bones desiccated by a million, million years of fire and ice.

Those who walk in the shadow of Mawenzi walk on tiptoe; and speak, if they dare speak at all, in whispers.

After Mawenzi your eyes fall on Kibo with relief. The west peak, a giant dome of white, seems serene and welcoming. Its soft contours caress the sky, not rend it. Its flowing glaciers and snowfields roll gently downwards, winking and shimmering in sun and moon alike. A benign, friendly peak, this highest place of Africa; soft sister to harsh Mawenzi.

Beware. It is a trick. The softness has claws; the velvet mask hides a stern face. In an instant the mask can be ripped away as the sun darkens and howling winds spring up and scour across the heights. Blizzards batter the vast slopes, piling snow on snow until the mountain can bear no more and mile-long snow-meadows groan with weight, creak and begin to move. Slowly at first, but building speed with every inch until they scream down the slopes, a million tons of suffocating bone-breaking white.

The mountain held no fear for Alan, it was too well-known for that. But familiarity had never brought complacency. He knew the mountain's dangers. Like the sea, it has moods, and if you know them you are safe.

So why now, sitting quietly in the warm sun, did he feel so anxious? He felt jittery and nervy, unaccountably fearful, of something he couldn't define. Something which was working on his heart not his brain.

His brain said that there was nothing to fear. From the mountain or Kimathi. Both were lifelong friends.

But his heart was telling him another story, though it was whispering it so low that he could hardly hear it. A small, urgent whisper which settled in his heart as a nagging doubt.

His brain said that Kilima Njaro was just the same; just as he had always known it.

His heart said that it was changed, subtly different in its aspect. Not as he remembered it.

Perhaps it was just that he had been away so long. Perhaps his eyes had become used to softer, smaller things; things of a different scale. It was he that was changed, not the mountain.

Or perhaps it was the urgency of his quest, the unknown danger Njombo had spoken of, that was painting the mountain in strange, disturbing colours.

These were the things he told himself.

But they gave him no reassurance. He didn't believe them.

The mountain *was* changed, but he couldn't say how. It seemed to loom more forbiddingly than he remembered, yet there was nothing about its aspect which would account for that.

He sat and looked at Kibo's great, rounded flanks,

trying to read what was there, to find some explanation for his disquiet.

But the mountain simply sat there.

Silent, eternally ice-bound, cold and austere, it lay like a sleeping beast caught in some strange, magic spell which suspended time, as well as rock, in ice.

That was it, Alan realized. That was what had been niggling him. It wasn't the face of the mountain which was changed, it was the feel of it. Expectancy hung on the air, like a shimmering curtain. The mountain was waiting.

Alan snorted to himself with annoyance and shook his head sharply. What nonsense. The altitude was affecting his brain. The height had unbalanced him. The brain cells can gasp for oxygen just as surely as the lungs can. He needed sleep. In the morning things would be back to normal.

He dismissed the silly thoughts and decided to go to bed. He picked up his rucksack, took one last look at Kibo, smiling at the tricks the mind can play, and then stepped into the hut.

Inside, a couple of exhausted climbers, early down from the summits, snoozed comfortably by the fire, wrapped snugly in their bulky anoraks, their woolly hats still on their heads. He tiptoed quietly past them and climbed the ladder into the long, narrow bunk-room. Even just this small effort made him gasp for breath and he had to stand still for a moment or two until the heaving of his lungs passed.

Then he selected a bunk near the door so that he could leave early in the morning without disturbing anyone. He took off his boots, unrolled his sleeping-bag on to the mattress, and climbed into it fully clothed.

The softness and warmth of the down bag was immensely welcoming. Very soon the aches and nausea began to recede and he fell into a deep and healing sleep.

In the late afternoon, as the parties of climbers began to wander in, heavy clouds started to mass in great, soaring battlements of grey around the summits.

Just after nightfall the snow began, blanketing Horombo in the unearthly silence which only snow can bring.

At about ten o'clock when all the climbers were secure in the glowing interiors of the huts, a long, spectral line of ghostly warriors emerged from below, passed, silent and unnoticed, through the shadows and melted upwards into the driving snow.

At midnight, when the fires had died, the hissing gas-lamps had been extinguished and Horombo slept, two solitary figures followed them.

An old man in an earth-red robe, leaning heavily on a tall, forked stick.

And a boy, dragging a painful, wounded leg.

nineteen

John Edwards was stunned by what Sebastian Makayowe was telling him. It was almost beyond belief.

'Are you sure?' he asked, his voice hoarse with shock.

'Sure!' replied Makayowe. 'The village is deserted. They've all gone up on to the mountain. I'm sure of it.'

'But why? Why would they single Alan out? He's only a boy. What has he ever done to them?'

'Bwana, these are simple people. They believe what they are told to believe. They believe in signs, in magic. For some reason Alan is the one they want.'

'Damn,' John Edwards exclaimed. 'How could I have been so stupid. I should never have left him alone out here. I even told him to go looking for Kimathi to find out what was happening. But I meant look for him in the village. I didn't expect him to go up there, on the mountain.'

'Don't blame yourself, bwana, you couldn't have known.'

'Sebastian,' Mary Edwards spoke very quietly. 'Alan and Kimathi were born on the same day. Do you think that's the connection?' Her face was white with anxiety.

'Perhaps. Whatever it is we have to find him quickly.' Makayowe reached out and took Mary Edwards's hand. There was nothing else to do to help her in her distress. She knew, as well as they, what Makayowe meant. 'Find him or he dies.'

'Find him?' John Edwards slumped heavily into a chair. 'How in heaven's name are we going to find him?'

The problem of locating Alan on a mountain the size of Kilima Njaro defeated him.

'We have to find him,' his wife whispered. 'We have to.'

Makayowe, as usual, was far from defeated.

'Come,' he said. 'We will waste no more time. We will go to Moshi now and I will have a helicopter brought from Dar es Salaam. With that we will find him. Please, bwana, pack some clothes quickly, we may have to go high on the mountain.'

'Right.' John Edwards hurried out of the room, immediately cheered by the thought that there was a chance.

'Mama Edwards,' Makayowe turned to Mary, 'you too will pack some clothes. Tonight you will stay at the Moshi Hotel. I do not think you are in danger here, but you will be closer to us if you need us.'

'Very well, Sebastian.'

'Quickly, we go.'

And within minutes the commander had bundled

his friends into the Landcruiser and they were roaring down the hill to Moshi.

John Edwards sat staring at the windscreen throughout the journey but saw nothing through it. His eyes were turned inwards upon his own guilt. This was his fault, he was certain of it.

If only he had been honest with Alan, instead of making light of everything, then the boy would still be at home where he could be protected.

He had never suspected that it was Alan who was in the greatest peril. He had known there was danger, of course. He was not a fool. Tribal cults are deadly, he knew that. And from the first discovery of the sacrificial chicken he had known that the farm was marked. But he had believed the danger to be more to himself than to his family; some revenge on him for a long-borne grudge or imagined injustice.

And he had believed the danger to be containable, trusting Sebastian Makayowe to allow no harm to come to them, so there had been no point in alarming his wife and son.

Now, because of his thoughtlessness, his son was up there on the mountain walking unsuspectingly to his death.

All he could do now was pray that they would find the boy in time.

twenty

Kimathi and WaChui approached Leopard Point just after dawn.

The snow had stopped but a dense, white mist swirled down the mountain. It played tricks with the eyes. Momentarily the path would be there then, in a blink of the eye, it was gone. Dark buttresses of rock, banded and dusted with white powder, would loom out of the mist then, as rapidly as they came, recede. As though the very rocks stepped forward, hesitated, then stepped back again.

Sometimes the red-robed figure in front of Kimathi would be swallowed entirely, as if suddenly absorbed by the mountain. Then he would emerge again, higher, still struggling, his bony legs driving him ever upwards.

Kimathi's leg hurt terribly now, in spite of the healing poultice the old man had applied. The punishment asked of it had been too great. They had been walking without stop for sixteen hours and now his leg throbbed searingly and felt twice its size. Time and time again he thought he could go no further; wished he could lie down in the snow and abandon this terrible, fearful journey.

But the Song would not let him go.

The Song drove his legs, drew him onwards step by painful step. He climbed now as though in a dream, hardly seeing the mountain, not recognizing the long-familiar places that he passed. He saw only the small piece of earth in front of him, where his next weary foot would fall. Each step demanded a superhuman effort to raise the leg, move it forward and let it fall again.

The Song was all around him, and now, as they approached its source, seemed to be inside him too. As though he, the mountain and the Song were one thing, inseparable from each other.

But not yet completely. A tiny, doubtful part of himself still remained outside, looking on.

What would the Song finally ask of him?

Would he be able to answer its demands?

He glanced upwards. The old man had disappeared again, melted into the mist.

Kimathi quickened his pace, using his spear as a stick, leaning heavily on it with each alternate step to lift the weight from his stabbing calf.

He rose up through a deep cleft in the rocks, just wide enough to allow the passage of a man. The clack of the spear shaft echoed around the cleft, its sound bouncing back and magnified by the ice-sheathed walls. He hurried through, oppressed by its looming narrowness.

He emerged on to a patch of jumbled scree. The path led across it, following the contour of the mountain, and then started to rise again to a second cleft, a huge gash in a buttress which soared upwards in dizzying immensity to the crater rim.

137

Here the old man was waiting, his red-robed figure insubstantial in the shifting mist. The warriors were there too, black and silent as the rocks themselves, ranged like ghost-sentries in front of the gashed rock.

An outcrop of jagged, tooth-like boulders lay, haphazardly, against the buttress wall.

Leopard Point. They had arrived.

Kimathi sat down on a stone, resting his wounded leg and suppressing his fear. His heart was beating wildly. He took deep breaths and held them, willing his heart to slow.

WaChui stepped forward and approached the buttress, to where a huge, blank slab of rock leaned against it. He signalled to the warriors.

With slow, dream-like motion they moved from their places and assembled at the slab. Then, simultaneously, they took hold of it and began to heave against it.

At the first push nothing happened.

The men grunted with the effort, relaxed briefly, then pushed again. The muscles bulged in their arms and legs, ripples of strain rolled down their backs and into their legs, and they gave, in unison, another mighty groan.

The slab creaked and, with a grinding scrape of stone on stone, began to move. An inch only; then it stopped.

The men relaxed, repositioned themselves, and heaved again. Another creak; another grind; another inch.

And again and again, grunting and heaving, until they gradually inched the slab to one side.

It revealed a deep, narrow crack in the buttress face.

Kimathi watched, his heart pounding. Behind the blackness he could see a faint, luminous glow emanating from deep inside the cleft. He stood and began to walk towards it, drawn by it like a moth to a lamp.

The world seemed to be whirling around him. His body felt strangely insubstantial, as though he were floating. But, as he approached the eerie light he found that the fear and doubt and pain were beginning to recede. A warmth began to suffuse him, rising up through his feet and numbing the agony of his wounded leg.

Things started to feel right.

The warriors drew back from the entrance as he approached and he passed between them.

WaChui turned and stepped into the narrow passageway.

Kimathi followed.

Together they descended towards the cave of the Leopard Spirit.

twenty-one

Alan knew that it had snowed as soon as he opened his eyes.

Snow deadens the air.

The voices of the porters as they prepared breakfast floated in from outside as through cotton wool. The sharp clink of metal cooking pots and the crackle of the fires were muffled.

Alan lay in the warm depths of his sleeping-bag, listening.

He was cured of his sickness. His limbs had stopped aching and he felt relaxed and comfortable. The long, deep sleep had healed him, and his body had adjusted to the height. He was fine.

He eased himself reluctantly out of his sleeping-bag and swung his feet on to the floor. The air inside the hut was very chill and his boots, as he slipped his feet into them, were hard with the cold. He laced them carefully and tightly.

He stood and stretched, pushing the sleep out of his limbs. Then he walked over to the window and rubbed the frost from the panes.

The world outside was all white. The snow was no longer falling but the clouds had not yet lifted. The air hung grey and heavy, blocking his view of the steeply descending slopes. He opened the window and put his head out, breathing the sharp crispness of the morning air to clear his head.

Kibo was enveloped in dense cloud. The storm was still raging up there.

A porter passed by below, glanced upwards at the sound of the window opening, and called out to Alan.

'No climb today, bwana. Too much snow.'

Alan nodded back to him and pulled the window shut.

The guides had closed the mountain. It happened sometimes, when the weather was bad around the summits.

But it wouldn't affect him. Guides' rules were for tourists, not for him. The tourists didn't know what to expect on the mountain and would become disorientated and frightened on the snow-swept icescapes. They would start to wander off the paths, panic, go round in circles and be a danger to themselves and their long-suffering guides and porters.

Alan would go on anyway. He could walk the saddle blindfold, he had travelled it so many times. Whatever the conditions he would be able to get to Kibo Hut, just below the dome. Then he could reassess the weather there.

He returned to his bunk, rolled up his sleeping-bag and stuffed it into his rucksack. Then he climbed down the ladder into the lower room.

The climbers were grumbling amongst themselves, disappointed that they were unable to go on.

They milled about, disconsolate and aimless, waiting for the porters to bring breakfast.

A big cauldron of black tea was simmering on a crackling fire and Alan took his mug from his rucksack and dipped it in. The liquid was bitter and steeped in smoke, but it burned welcomely down his throat and into his stomach. He zipped up his anorak, crossed to the door and stepped outside. The morning air cut into his face and he hurried round the back of the huts to the cooking-sheds.

In the smoky depths the porters were cooking huge pans of porridge.

'Karibu, bwana. Help yourself,' said a smiling cook. 'Baridi sana, bwana. It is very cold.'

'Very,' replied Alan. 'Thank you for this.'

He took a plateful and went back outside. He sat on the steps of the main hut, out of the wind, and planned what to do.

It was seven o'clock. Walking steadily, avoiding the trap of hurry, he would be at Kibo Hut by eleven. Kimathi might even be there, at the hut, sheltering from the storm which was boiling around Kibo.

He watched the clouds obliterating the dome. Gusted by wind, they moved fitfully, angrily, billowing like thick smoke. But the foreboding Alan had felt yesterday was gone, now that he felt well again. He was confident, exhilarated even, by the new challenge of the weather.

He returned his empty plate to the cooking-shed, thanked the porters again and went back to the hut to collect his rucksack. The snow squelched beneath his boots. It was already softening as the day began to warm. Snow never lasted long this low down.

He carried his rucksack out of the hut and waited until he was sure there were no guides watching. If they saw him leave they would try to dissuade him from going further and he preferred not to argue with them.

When he was sure the coast was clear, he slipped away through the huts and started to ascend the long slope to the saddle.

He paused a second, puzzled, as he began to climb.

All around the flat clearing where the huts stood the snow was crisscrossed with tracks of deep boot-prints, where the climbers, guides and porters had come and gone on their early morning ventures.

But on the slope, in front of him, a very clear double track of trampled snow rose upwards and disappeared into the swirling clouds above. More snow had fallen on the tracks but they were still, quite clearly, lines of footprints.

Someone had passed this way in the night, walking while the snow still fell.

He looked again at the prints, but they were too indistinct for him to decide whether the feet had been climbing or descending. He decided it must have been the latter. No one would climb up over the saddle at night and in snow. It was a party of climbers, down late from the tops, who had arrived after nightfall.

He dismissed the tracks and continued to climb.

Half an hour later he was on the saddle.

There, unprotected by the lee of the mountain, he

found the snow was still falling, driven towards him by a biting wind howling down from the peaks. He pulled his anorak hood up, tied it tightly around his face so that only his eyes showed, bent himself into the wind and began the long slow ascent towards Kibo.

He did not hear the twanging clatter of the police helicopter which passed a few hundred feet below him, hovered briefly at Horombo while its passengers jumped out, then roared away again down the Mweka Gully back to Moshi.

Two very grim-faced men jumped down from the helicopter.

As soon as their feet touched the ground they were running across the clearing towards the huts, hoping against hope that they would be in time to find Alan there.

John Edwards pounded through each of the huts in turn, shouting Alan's name and urgently hurling questions at startled climbers. Makayowe ran round to the back of the huts and rounded up the guides and porters.

Within minutes they had established that they were too late. They had missed him. And no one had seen him go.

John Edwards cursed.

Luck seemed to have been against them since yesterday. The helicopter had not been available when they rang and it had not arrived until dusk, much too late to attempt the dangerous flight up the mountain.

They had spent the night at Moshi police station

then, at first light, they had begun the flight which had led them here. Too late.

If only the cloud had not been so low they could still have found him. If the mountain had been clear above Horombo the helicopter could have risen up to the saddle and they would have located him within minutes.

Now all they could do was follow on foot.

Makayowe shouted.

'Over here, Bwana John.'

He had found Alan's footprints, a clear line leaving the haphazardly trampled snow and ascending towards the saddle.

John Edwards joined him.

In seconds they were gone, their heavily clad, bulky figures melting into the low clouds.

twenty-two

The sun began to disperse the clouds at about ten o'clock.

Alan was high up on the saddle by then, approaching Kibo. He had felt the wind lessening for the past mile as it blew itself out. He had found, gradually, that he hadn't needed to bend so far into it and now could walk almost upright.

The snowfall had started to ease too. The big, heavy flakes which had whipped at him since leaving Horombo had become smaller and smaller until they were now merely swirls of harmlessly gusting white powder.

As the cloud cover became less dense Alan had brief, tantalizing flashes of blue sky or white mountain, viewed as through a window with curtains of mist hanging at its sides.

He emerged at last into sunlight, and untied his hood and pushed it back from his face. He felt liberated as the cold air flowed over his face and through his hair. The air smelled magical; crisp and clean and pure. He breathed in deeply, filling his lungs with the breath of the mountain.

He turned and looked back down the way he had come. The mountain below was hidden in a vast sea of cotton wool. He seemed to be floating, sailing in the sky, borne on the back of Kibo high above the world.

Far, far in the distance Mawenzi's spires, tinged pink by the hazy sun, reached up through the fleece and tried to grasp the sky.

He turned again and carried on walking.

Kibo peak loomed over him now. He was approaching the lower flank of its great ice-dome, climbing steadily on to its final reaches. Ahead of him the pillars of Bismarck Towers rose like silent sentinels guarding the way to Uhuru Peak, still two thousand feet above his head. He could see a thin plume of smoke circling upwards from the dying breakfast fires at Kibo Hut, and snaking down the saddle, far in the distance, the bright clothes of descending climbers drew a line of colour on the glaring whiteness of the snow.

He scanned the flanks of the mountain, trying to decide where to look for Kimathi.

He could try the hut first; the snowfall could have driven his friend to take shelter there. But Kimathi wouldn't stay there long, Alan decided. He was here with a purpose, Njombo had told him that. Whatever it was he was looking for he wouldn't find it in a cheerless, stone hut filled with climbers.

Alan cast his mind back to the things Njombo had said. Perhaps the words contained a clue, a hidden message which the old man had been too afraid to say outright.

He turned the words over again in his mind, trying to make sense of them.

Perhaps it was some sort of tribal initiation that Kimathi was undergoing.

'The Kimathi you knew is no more. The boy is gone. Now the man must tread another path.'

All tribes have some ceremony, some test, which marks the moment when a boy takes his place with the men, proves his fitness to be one of them. But this, Alan thought, was a strange test. Boys usually had to prove they could fight or hunt effectively, to protect and feed their people.

What could Kimathi be proving up here? There was nothing to hunt up here, nothing to conquer. The only enemy was the mountain itself; and then only if you, yourself, made it so.

So it was more than just a test of strength.

'Kimathi has gone to the mountain to bring us a sign,' Njombo had said.

Alan knew well that Kilima Njaro had a mystical significance for all the teeming tribes which lived in its great shadow. There was no surprise in that. The vastness and majesty of this mountain could not fail to affect anyone who gazed upon it; it dwarfed everything else into insignificance. Its great bulk had risen at the beginnings of time and it would still be there, silently watching, at the end. How could man not look at this mountain and feel that here was eternity?

Ngàje Ngài the Maasai called it. The House of God. Eternal as God himself.

But that was the Maasai. What the Chagga believed about the mountain Alan had no idea. Kimathi had never spoken about it.

'A time of magic,' Njombo had said.

Perhaps Kimathi was seeking the magic.

But where?

Alan scanned the heights. The answer was there somewhere, in the mountain. There to read, if you could see it. In the heights of Uhuru Peak or the faces of the Breschen Wall; hiding deep in Hans Meyer Cave; at cold Gillman's, or the lonely, jutting teeth of Leopard Point.

Alan stopped short in his steps, pulled up by a sudden thought.

Leopard.

Leopard Point.

The answer was there.

Of course. How could he have been so stupid? Why had he not made the connection before?

The word CHUI scrawled in blood on the shed wall.

Leopard.

In a stabbing flash of realization it was clear. He had thought the word to be a threat, a warning. Njombo's words had threatened danger so Alan had tried to explain the strange event in those terms, perhaps part of a tribal ritual to drive them away, a simple act of defiance or revenge for some long-harboured hurt.

But it hadn't been a threat. Alan knew now what it had been. The word had been a direction, a signpost, pointing him this way. Unknowingly, subconsciously, he had obeyed an order. The word CHUI had drawn him up the mountain, was pointing him to Leopard Point.

His brain whirled as he took in the thought.

He was *meant* to be here.

Alan's confidence flowed away. The hand which had scrawled that word, with brutal coarseness, had been Kimathi's hand. Kimathi, his lifelong companion, his friend from birth, was summoning him.

Why?

Alan tried to rationalize his sudden dread.

'No harm could ever come to me from Kimathi.' That was what he had told himself as he had started out on his journey. Now, in the great silences of Kilima Njaro, he was not so sure.

Could it be? Could it possibly be that Kimathi was changed, as everyone else seemed to be changed?

No. He couldn't believe that. Not Kimathi.

But, if he didn't believe it, why was he so afraid? In an instant of realization the face of the mountain had transformed into something sinister and menacing.

The feeling he had had yesterday returned, stronger than before.

The mountain *was* expectant. It *was* waiting.

He had the overwhelming feeling that he was being watched. That something lurked, invisible in the high whitenesses of the peaks, watching him with hungry, waiting eyes.

Suddenly danger stalked the snow.

Fear told him to turn and run, to get away from this place.

He tried to turn, but found that he could not. His eyes were drawn inexorably up to Leopard Point. The rest of the mountain became indistinct, shadowed at the sides of his vision, as though he saw through a misted tunnel. Only Leopard Point was clear.

His legs began to move, without him willing them to. He felt strangely disembodied, as though walking in a dream.

And, as he walked, he seemed to hear a haunting music, soft at first but building with each step.

A sweet, insistent melody which drew him, steadily and surely, up to the white heights of Leopard Point.

twenty-three

The slab had concealed a long, raking passage of pure ice, ghostly luminous and searingly cold. As Kimathi followed the old man down it their footfalls whispered eerily back to them in soft echoes from the walls. The light gradually became stronger as they descended until, finally, they emerged into an immense ice-cavern.

They were deep in the glacier, in a vast air-bubble caught and frozen to eternity a million, million years ago.

Here the air danced as light permeated the glacial roof above them and was reflected, blindingly, from a thousand soaring ice-pillars. Huge, rearing stalactites and stalagmites made a petrified forest of ice-trees.

WaChui stopped and signalled the boy to pass him.

Kimathi laid his spear on the ground, unrolled his bundle of leopard skins, and put them on.

Then, with the light catching the black and gold of the pelts, he began to walk towards the centre of the cavern. He moved now with certainty.

The old man watched carefully. As the boy passed between the ice-columns his outline became indistinct, shifting and reforming, subtly changed as he advanced.

The Song was changing too. Kimathi could feel it seeping down into the pores of his skin. He was drowning in the Song.

And he was changing as he drowned. A power began to creep through him, the power of agile, easy strength, as though his legs could carry him at the speed of the wind for ever. He seemed freed from the limits of a clumsy wounded body. Built of air.

'The Leopard runs alone,' sang the Song. 'Run as the Leopard and hear its Song.'

'I have heard it,' said Kimathi, in his mind.

'The Leopard kills in darkness; kill as the Leopard and be the Song.'

'I have killed,' Kimathi whispered. 'I am the Song.'

The Song continued.

'I am the Spirit. I am everywhere, everything. I am He. I am the sun and stars, the world and time. I am you and you are me. I am existence, eternal and changeless. I am creation. I decide.'

The words bored into Kimathi. The ice-cavern seemed now to be spinning around him. Dizzy, he fell to his knees, hands pressed to the floor.

'Now it is your time. The time of the Leopard. You, guardian of my spirit on earth, now you must prove yourself. The sacrifice approaches. Go now. And kill.'

As the words echoed around inside his head, Kimathi had a brief, lightning flash of realization.

He gasped.

He saw a picture of a lone, small figure, bent

against the moaning wind and driving snow, struggling across the grey desolation of the saddle. A figure Kimathi knew so well that there could be no possibility of mistake.

But, before the terror of what he had to do could take hold of him, the picture faded and was replaced by a terrible longing. His eyes, burning yellow now, grew wider and glazed into a fixed, hate-filled stare.

He growled quietly and licked his fangs, lips drawn back in the cat-snarl of a hungry predator.

The ache was back. The undeniable ache of hunger in the throat.

Blood hunger.

He turned, a single thought only now filling his mind.

The kill.

He padded silently back across the cavern and into the passageway.

twenty-four

'Yes,' said one of the party of climbers, in answer to the question, 'there was one person coming up. We could see him as we started down from the hut, but he turned off long before we got near to him. He went over in that direction. If you go on a bit you'll see his tracks in the snow, going off to the left.'

John Edwards and Commander Makayowe had emerged from the cloud line just as the climbers were descending into it.

'We were going to tell him not to bother,' continued the climber. 'The snow's too heavy to reach the summit today. The guides say that it's too dangerous. He turned off before we could tell him, though.'

And the climbers continued their steady descent, their voices soon lost, muted by the deadening clouds.

'Thank God,' said John Edwards, as he and the commander hurried on. 'At least we know he's still alive. There's a chance yet. And at least we can see now.'

'Yes,' replied Makayowe. 'When we get up over the next rise we might even be able to see him. Talk no more, bwana. Save your lungs. Climb.'

And they continued upwards, attacking the steep rise with hurried steps.

Ten minutes later they surfaced, gasping in the thin air, over the top of the slope.

Hurriedly Makayowe pulled his powerful binoculars from their case, clipped on the darkened-glass lens covers against the blinding snow, and began to scan the mountain. He swept the glasses across the barren snowfields ahead of them, found Alan's tracks and followed them. The tracks led right up to the foot of Bismark Towers.

Makayowe nodded to himself. His hunch had been right. He knew where the boy was going. He moved the binoculars a little to the right and started to scan up the deep gully of Johannes Notch.

Sure enough, the boy was there, a small, bright splodge of colour against the vast expanse of white.

'I've found him, Bwana John. He's there. He's all right. Still climbing.'

'Thank God,' whispered John Edwards.

Makayowe started to return the binoculars to their case, fumbling clumsily with frozen fingers.

Behind him he heard a soft, metallic click. The small sound of a safety catch.

'No,' he bellowed, whirling around with such violence that he startled the other man, freezing him in the very act of firing his rifle into the air.

'What's the matter?' asked John Edwards, his finger still on the trigger. 'I was going to fire to bring him back. He'll know it's a warning and turn round.'

'Bwana,' sighed Makayowe, 'look at the mountain.

It groans with snow. Fire here and you will kill us all. Alan as well.'

John Edwards looked up at the dome of Kibo. Immense snowfields blanketed every slope, hung over every gully, teetered, finely balanced, over every wall.

Ashamed at his stupidity he started to apologize, but Makayowe cut him off.

'Come, bwana, quickly. We go. Alan is climbing in Johanne's Notch. It is very steep and very slow. We will take the tourist route up to Hans Meyer Cave. That is the easiest way and much quicker. Then we can cut across the mountain. With luck we will meet Alan as he comes out of the gully. Come now. There is still time.'

His great legs began to pump away, over the level expanse of snow which stretched, unbroken for two miles, across to the path which led up the final slopes of Kibo.

John Edwards shouldered his rifle and hurried after him, praying that the man's words were right.

'There is still time,' he repeated, over and over again in his mind, willing it to be true. 'There is still time.'

twenty-five

The gully was desperately steep and the air desperately thin.

Alan's vision swam with dizziness as he looked up the narrow cleft knifing into the sky.

His lungs rasped at each step, and now he could go no more than six paces at a time. Then he would stop, gasping deeply for minutes on end, until his heart had slowed enough to release his legs for the next six steps.

Sometimes he thought that he could go no further; that his legs would buckle beneath him and his lungs would burst.

But always he went on. The strange, haunting music drew him on. He had no fear of it, or of the mountain from which it came. He was Alan Edwards no longer. His past life had faded from his mind.

He only knew that it was right that he was on this mountain. That he should be there. And that he had to go on.

That was the only thought left in his deeply entranced mind.

Go on. On to the source of the music. Become a part of its magic.

And so he climbed, body wracked with effort, but mind filled with a single, shining thought.

And above him the leopard paced, raging with impatience, mouth redly salivating, with his own single thought.

They met, finally, in the place they had always been meant to meet. The place decreed at their births.

The boy rose up through the dark, ice-bound rocks of the cleft and on to the silent moonscape of the screes. The sun had eased around the mountain and was slipping behind a buttress of rock. The jagged rocks of Leopard Point lay in deep shadow and the entrance to the cave yawned blackly. The painted warriors stood, as before, ranged like statues, spears at rest, silent and still as the mountain slopes.

Above them, high on the scree, the leopard swung back and forth, snarling and spitting, on an invisible pendulum of rage.

As the boy appeared the leopard stood still. It froze, its muscles locked in the terrible cat-stillness which precedes the final chase and the kill.

The boy saw none of this.

He saw a different landscape, its colours painted by his Song-drugged mind; a place of quiet beauty, calm and friendly after the oppressive gully.

The air here was filled with the music.

Away across the slope a soft light beckoned him from a cave-mouth, a welcoming lantern calling a weary traveller.

His journey was over. He had reached the source of the music.

He was home.

He began to walk towards the light, smiling with happiness. He saw nothing else.

The warriors turned their sightless eyes towards him.

And the leopard padded slowly, inexorably, with delicate cat-precision, down the scree towards the boy.

A few hundred yards to the left John Edwards and Sebastian Makayowe rounded the icefield directly below Gillman's Point and stopped.

Makayowe hissed, a sharp intake of breath, as he quickly took in the scene below; the boy walking calmly towards the cave-mouth; the warriors motionless, waiting; the leopard poised, muscles tensed, on a rock a few feet above the boy.

For a second John Edwards was frozen with horror by the scene. Involuntarily he shouted out to his son; a harsh, terror-filled cry.

The boy seemed not to hear and continued his slow walk towards the cave. In a few seconds he would pass directly below the leopard, and nothing then would stop the animal launching itself through the air in its final, murderous leap.

There was no time for rational thought. The heavy hunting-rifle was at John Edwards's shoulder and ready to fire as if it had leapt there by itself. Dropping to his knees he rested the barrel on a stone and scanned the telescopic sight across the rocks of Leopard Point.

This time Makayowe did not stop him, though he

looked anxiously up the slopes above the boy to the deep snowfields massed at the summits.

The leopard slid into the sights and John Edwards increased the pressure very slightly on the trigger, centring the sight precisely on the animal's heart.

The leopard was crouched now, its point of balance slightly back from centre. It was on the point of hurling itself upon the boy.

He pulled the trigger at the exact moment that the leopard's legs began to uncoil and launch it into the air.

The bullet missed the heart but thudded heavily into the spine.

The leopard spun in mid-air and crashed to the ground, where it lay writhing. A long, rending howl of rage and pain rose from the animal, mingling with the high, cracking echoes of the gunshot.

Alan's head swung round at the sound. For a second he was caught between two worlds. The sun-filled light began to dim as he hovered between sleep and waking.

Then he awoke, to a terrible, bewildering nightmare. He felt his legs go weak as he tried to comprehend what he now saw. His mind screamed at the sight of the ranks of silent warriors, their blank eyes staring at him.

He heard a voice calling him, but it seemed a thousand miles away. A faint, but urgent, cry drifted into the clearing.

'Alan,' it called. 'Run, Alan. Run.'

But the horror stopped him moving.

His eyes flicked from the warriors to the leopard.

It was facing away from him, the glowing gold and black of its pelt seeming to shine in the cold light. Blood seeped down from its hind leg and painted a startling pool of colour on the white snow.

High above him he heard the mountain groan, and felt its tremor deep beneath his feet.

'Run,' the voice called. 'RUN!'

But he remained rooted to the spot, his eyes fixed in horrified disbelief on the leopard.

It stopped its agonizing writhing and lay still for a second. It growled softly to itself.

Then, with infinite slowness, it began to move.

Grunting with pain it pushed itself up into a sitting position, then slowly dragged itself round until it faced the boy.

It sat, head hanging low, mouth open to suck great, shallow gasps of air.

It tried to stand, but its back end trailed uselessly on the ground and refused to rise. It snarled angrily, its mind still intent on the kill. Hatred poured from its eyes, a hatred which chilled Alan as he watched the mortally wounded beast make one last, desperate effort to reach him.

It began to pull itself forward by its front legs, its broken body sliding uselessly behind it in the snow.

And then, suddenly, a second shot cracked out.

The leopard shuddered as the heavy bullet slammed into its chest, then it became still; the stillness of deep, mortal shock.

Overhead, high above them, the mountain rumbled again. For a moment only, Alan took his eyes off the leopard and looked up. The snowfields seemed to tremble as they reverberated with the rolling echoes of the shot.

When Alan looked back at the leopard it lay crouched, breathing very shallowly, its head resting on its legs. It was very close to death.

Its eyes were still fixed on Alan, but the terrible rage was beginning to dim. The fires of blood-lust had died in them and instead, as Alan watched the animal's final moments, the eyes seemed bewildered, dismayed and deeply afraid.

It blinked once, as though trying to clear its vision, then stared hard again at Alan.

Alan stared back, fascinated, and saw, for a brief second only, a softening in the animal's eyes. A tiny flicker only, but unmistakable. A flicker of recognition.

It faded swiftly and the leopard died.

In the deep silence which followed it felt to Alan that the mountain held its breath; that the world's heart missed a beat.

Then the mountain began to live again.

A long, grinding groan began to murmur through Alan's feet and into his legs, like the beginnings of an earthquake deep in the ground.

A soft, hissing sound from high above on the trembling slopes began to whisper insistently on the air.

He looked up.

Creaking, inch by inch, barely perceptibly, the great snowfields were beginning to move.

Frantic voices penetrated Alan's consciousness.

'Alan. Run, boy. Run. Avalanche. Get away. GET AWAY!'

Panic flowed through him and released his legs. He turned quickly. The whole slope above him was on the move now, roaring dully as it gathered momentum. He could see the snow beginning to ripple and break into clouds of white spume.

He started to run back the way he had come, trying to reach the cleft in the buttress at the entrance to Leopard Point.

The sound of the avalanche was deafening now as it approached. A tremendous storm of snow battered its way down the mountain, sweeping rocks and ice-slabs away in its path. From the corner of his eye Alan could see it bearing down upon him, a huge wall of white, like an immense wave curling upwards ready to crash down on him and drown him.

At the last second he threw himself into the gash in the buttress and crouched, trembling, in its lee.

The roar became a great, interminable crashing. The whole mountain shook and rattled and hammered around him as the avalanche swept past. Driven snow billowed into the cleft and choked him as he lay huddled and quivering.

And then, miraculously, it began to pass. The crashings lessened, the roaring dulled, diminished and faded away as the snow-sea poured down the ice-slopes, precipices and gullies of Kibo to die in vast white clouds on the slopes of the saddle.

It was over. He had survived.

He sat for a moment, still trembling, to let his fear

abate. Then he stood, brushed the covering of blown snow from his clothes and stepped out of the cleft.

Away over the distant slopes below Gillman's Point he could see two brightly clad figures waiting for him.

He waved once, then started to walk towards them.

epilogue

When the storms had passed and the warm African sun melted the snows on the saddle, the mountain gave up its dead.

The Chagga warriors were brought down and buried at Marangu village. Their wives and children wept and mourned them. Then, shortly after, they left. The village was deserted.

The old man who watched over the tree was never seen again and, if there had been anyone left to look, they would have seen that the great tree which towered above his cave slowly withered and died.

John Edwards and his family returned to the farm and tried to resume their lives. Gradually new workers appeared and the coffee slopes rang to the sound of voices once more.

Njombo simply walked away into the bush and died. Perhaps of heartbreak, perhaps of shame. Perhaps of something else.

Alan never climbed Kilima Njaro again.

The body of Kimathi was never found. But then no one who had lived these events expected it to be.

Some years later a party of climbers, lost in the mist and well off the normal mountain routes, came across the frozen carcass of a leopard, wedged in a cleft in the rocks as though it had been thrown there, its body embedded in ice.

Kiswahili words used in this book

asante thank you

bwana mister/sir

chai tea

chui leopard

habari? how are you?

jambo hello

kanga length of cloth which women wrap around themselves as a dress

karibu welcome to . . .

mzee (pron. um-zay) respected elder gentlemen

mzuri I'm fine

pombe local beer (usually made from maize)

sana very/much (e.g. *asante sana* . . . thank you very much; *baridi sana* . . . very cold)

ugali maize-meal, porridge